WARRIOR

Douglas Hill is a Ca[...]
several years. He bec[...]
early age – by reading comics like *Flash Gordon* – and has
remained a hopeless addict ever since. In the sixties he
began reviewing science fiction regularly for *Tribune*, at a
time when the national press barely acknowledged the
existence of sf. He is now Literary Editor of *Tribune*, has
also written many short stories and compiled sf
anthologies.

His *Last Legionary* quartet has been called 'the best kids'
SF of the last decade' (*Books for Keepers*).

Warriors of the Wasteland is the sequel to *The Huntsman*
and continues the story of Finn Ferral and his struggle
against the Alien Slavers.

DOUGLAS HILL

Warriors of the Wasteland

PICCOLO BOOKS

in association with Heinemann

For MICHAEL again
who helped with this one too

First published 1983 by William Heinemann Ltd
This Piccolo edition published 1984 by Pan Books Ltd,
Cavaye Place, London SW10 9PG
in association with William Heinemann Ltd

9 8 7 6 5 4 3 2

© Douglas Hill 1983

ISBN 0 330 28452 5

Printed and bound in Great Britain by
Hunt Barnard Printing Ltd, Aylesbury, Bucks.

Contents

PART ONE

Creatures of The Claw

1

Capture

THE SMALL BATWINGED creature drifted through the empty sky, its bulging eyes tirelessly scanning the land below. Around it, on every side, jagged mountain peaks thrust up like gigantic broken teeth, with snow still glistening on some of them though it was late summer. Directly below the flying creature, between two spiky crests, lay a broad sweep of uplands, rising in an easy slope, richly covered in evergreens and scrub brush. As the creature swooped lower, to peer more closely into the shadows among the greenery, a rust-feathered hawk flung itself up from a treetop, as if to challenge the intruder. But then the hawk veered suddenly away, plunging back into cover even more swiftly than it had risen.

The hawk had sensed that the batwinged creature was not truly alive. Though it was partly flesh and blood, of a kind, its eyes were made of a clear, hard substance like transparent metal, and within the small dark body were other delicate mechanisms of metal. Those mechanisms transmitted, over astonishing distances, images of whatever the creature was seeing – images that appeared on large, oddly-coloured screens, surrounded by complex and strangely-shaped controls.

And the eyes that studied those screens, the hands that touched the controls to guide the creature's flight, were not human.

But back on the forested uplands it was a very human figure

that stepped out of a thicket, after the flying creature had vanished into the distance. It was a young man, no more than twenty, compactly muscled, who wore a sleeveless jerkin, trousers and low boots all made from animal hide. A heavy knife hung at one hip, a belt-pouch at the other; a strip of leather that was a sling was wrapped round his left wrist. He stood statue-still, sniffing the light breeze that ruffled his straw-coloured hair, his clear grey eyes warily surveying the sky.

The young man's name was Finn Ferral. Once he had lived carefree and contented, as the huntsman for a tiny village huddled deep in an eastern forest. But that village was now many months and many hundreds of kilometres behind him. From their home in the village Finn's family had been forcibly taken, carried off into terror and torment. And since then Finn had crossed more than half a continent, in a relentless, hazardous pursuit that few other humans in the world – as the world was – would have dared to begin.

Satisfied that the sky held no further danger, Finn turned back into the thicket. Though the brush was dense and dry, not a twig crackled, not a leaf rustled, as he wove his way among the branches. It was an effortless silence, almost instinctive, as if Finn was as much a wild animal as he was a human being. And the other figure, waiting for him in the depths of the thicket, seemed even more like a beast than a man.

He was no taller than Finn, but awesomely broader, a vast bulk of muscle. He wore only ragged trousers made of coarse cloth, and sturdy leather boots – but all of his massive upper body was covered in a dense, tangled pelt of light-coloured hair. And above one huge shoulder jutted the hilt of a machete, its sheath strapped against the mounded hump of muscle on his upper back.

His name was Baer, and he was one of a race of beings who called themselves the Bloodkin. They were descended from humans, in a chillingly unnatural way, but were closer to beasts – the beasts of nightmare and horror story – in their brutal savagery. Except for Baer. Far more of true humanity had been born in him: intelligence, compassion, humour. It was the human heart within Baer's fearsome body that had led him, long before, to break away from his own bestial kind – and eventually to meet Finn Ferral, and to join him in his grim quest.

Baer stepped forward, aware as always of how much noise he made in the wilderness, compared to his young companion.

"That's the second spywing this week," he said, in a rumbling, melodious bass. "Wish I knew what they're doin', out here in the middle of nothin'."

"Looking for us, maybe," Finn said with a smile.

"Not funny," Baer growled. "It could be. An' the idea makes me nervous."

Finn shrugged. "We've been hunted before. What's different?"

"Where we're goin' is what's different," Baer rumbled. "Past these mountains we'll be comin' to the edge of the Wasteland. Which means big open stretches of nothin'. We'll be as exposed as a black fox in a snowfield."

"And past the Wasteland," Finn replied firmly, "are more mountains. Which is where we're heading. Even if every spywing in the west wants to come and watch."

Baer tugged his great beard dourly. "I'm not sayin' we shouldn't keep goin'. I'm just sayin' things'll get worse 'fore they get better."

Then he grinned sheepishly as Finn burst out laughing.

"Folks in my village always used to say that," Finn said. "They were a gloomy lot, too." He jerked his head towards the west. "So let's go see how much worse things get."

He moved away through the brush, with Baer crashing noisily along behind him. "Just don't forget," Baer grumbled, "if we got spywings now, we maybe got somethin' a lot nastier not far behind."

Some days later, things had got worse. They were toiling through a region that made them long for the gentler slopes of the uplands. It was as if all the land in that part of the mountains had been squeezed and crumpled by some unimaginable force. The rocky terrain was split and broken – a series of ravines and steep-sided valleys, separated by barren tablelands. Yet there was still some plant life, mostly small twisted pine trees and thorny scrub. And among them, just as well adapted to that harsh world, many small animals found the means for survival. And where any wild creatures could live, so could Finn Ferral.

So he and Baer forged steadily on, through day after day of fierce exertion, of wind-swept ridges and rock-slabbed ravines, of high pale skies that remained empty of dark shapes with bat-wings.

Until a day came that brought to an end their time of uninterrupted travel.

The day was dwindling towards twilight, and as usual Finn had left Baer to make camp while he ranged out into the wilds. He was looking for water, to fill the leather water-bottle that Baer carried, and he was hunting, his sling ready in his hand, a sharp-edged stone from his belt-pouch set in its place.

But also, like any wild creature, he was prowling, making sure that no dangers lurked near the place where he would bed down for the night. So he was alert and watchful, listening to every fluttering leaf, sniffing the air like a wolf. And he drifted through the gathering shadows silent and unseen as a shadow himself.

The scent reached him first, and then the sound. A whiff of wood-smoke, followed by the almost inaudible murmur of voices. And if Finn had been a shadow before, now he was a ghost, vanishing into the brush as if the ground had swallowed him up.

Flat on his belly, he slid forward, towards the sounds. In moments he was close enough to peer cautiously past a low tangle of thorny branches.

Two Bloodkin. One of them lounging beside a small fire, the other standing upright, peering out into the gathering dusk. They were less bulky than Baer, but no less hairy. Both had long knives thrust into their belts, and their voices sounded harsh and angry. But then, Finn thought, Bloodkin always sounded angry about something.

" . . . so quit yer worryin'," the one by the fire was saying. "If The Claw says they're roun' here, then they're here. Them humans know these rocks. They'll sniff 'em out."

"Jus' the same," growled the one that was standing, "you heard what that kid c'n do. They c'd be sneakin' past right now."

The other snorted. "The kid's one thing, the renegade's another. We'd hear *him*. An' so'll them humans. They'll have 'em 'fore it's full dark. Why shouldn't we get some rest?"

"Mebbe," the standing Bloodkin grunted. "I'd jus' feel better if The Claw was here . . . "

His voice trailed away – but the menacing words were echoing and re-echoing in Finn's mind. He had no doubt that *he* was the "kid" they had spoke of, and Baer the "renegade", the Bloodkin who had deserted his own kind. But who or what was The Claw? And who were the humans who were somehow on his and Baer's trail? And, more important right then – *where* were they?

Finn felt a sick horror at the thought that humans might be working *with* the Bloodkin – serving the enemies of humanity, the Bloodkin's inhuman masters. He wanted to get back to Baer with all speed. But he also did not want to leave two armed Bloodkin lurking out in the wilds.

Smoothly he rose to his feet, the sling whirling. His own movement was soundless, but the faint hum of the sling caused the standing Bloodkin to turn his head with a puzzled frown.

He was still wearing the frown when the stone struck him precisely on the temple, and when he slumped to the ground beside the fire.

12

The other Bloodkin began scrambling astonishedly to his feet, but did not complete the movement. A second stone thudded meatily just between the close-set eyes, and he sprawled back on to the ground where he had lain.

Finn approached warily, knife ready. But neither of them moved – and by the look of the crushed temple of the first one, he would never move again. Finn reached for their knives and flung them into the darkness. He knew that he should probably finish off the second one, but he was not able to kill in cold blood, not even a Bloodkin. At least when the creature awoke he would be unarmed, and dazed for some time.

And by then Finn intended that he and Baer would be far away from this unsettling place, where humans willingly did the bidding of Bloodkin.

He sped away, his night vision quickly returning as he left the firelight behind. Swiftly he retraced his steps, knowing that Baer too would be sitting by a small fire, unaware of the dangers gathering round him in the darkness . . .

But at the end of his desperate dash, he found that he was too late.

There was a fire, and Baer was beside it. But he was lying full length, ominously still, the hair at the back of his head clotted with blood.

Finn crouched in the shadows, equal measures of fear and fury sweeping through him like a forest fire. His sensitive nostrils were aware of a combination of strange odours, including the rankness of human sweat, which told him that Baer must have been attacked by the humans that the two Bloodkin had talked about. But not even Finn's senses could tell him if the humans were skulking nearby, or if they had gone to search for him elsewhere, and had merely left their stink behind.

All of his wilderness instincts urged him to stay in hiding, to watch and wait. But his human mind and emotions told him to go to Baer's aid, to see if he still lived. He ghosted forward,

13

nervous as a hunted beast that suspects a trap it cannot see.

The whisper of sound brought him spinning around, snatching at his knife. But he was looking in the wrong place. The net settled over him, thick and knotted rawhide thongs, tangling his arms and legs so that he stumbled and fell as he tried, automatically, to leap away to safety.

And before he could begin to slash with his knife at the net's enveloping folds, there was a crashing in the underbrush around him, and seven evilly barbed spears were levelled at him where he lay.

2

People of the Gorge

AT ONCE FINN stopped his frantic struggles, and stared up at the men who held the spears. They were oddly garbed, in long, coarse-woven, stained robes, and they seemed unnaturally pale, as if they were creatures of darkness who rarely saw the sun.

"Here he be, Laslo," one of them said with a snigger. "Netted up like a new-caught fish."

He was talking to a man in the centre of the group – an older man, with leathery skin and grey, thinning hair, who wore a crude circle of metal like a pendant on a thong round his stringy neck.

"Praise the Great One," said the old man in a rasping voice. He stepped forward, looking down at Finn. "Young feller, the will of the Great One is bein' done here. Y' c'n bow to it, an' be nice an' peaceful. Or y' c'n try t' fight us, when we take the net off. But that'll jus' get y' a clout on the head like y'r pal there."

"Is he dead?" Finn asked through clenched teeth.

"Nope, he ain't," the rasping voice said. "But he can be, if y' don't keep y'rself quiet an' easy. What's it t' be?"

Relief washed through Finn like a tide, mingled with fear and caution. Baer was alive. But while he remained unconscious, and while Finn remained at the mercy of seven sharp spears, there was little choice. He had to do what they said, and bide his time.

"All right," he muttered.

"Praise the One," the old man said. He gestured to two of the others, and as they stooped to untangle the net from Finn the old man grinned gleefully, displaying a few stumps of yellowed teeth. "Boys, this's a night of great meanin'. There ain't nothin' The Claw won't give us when he gets hold of these two."

Finn did not resist as the robed men bound his arms behind him with strips of rawhide, and wound more rawhide round his legs. Baer was bound the same way, though he had not stirred. But within Finn rage and hatred were flaming, and as he watched the gloating smiles on the faces of his captors he could contain them no longer.

"Why are you people doing this?" he burst out at last. "We've done you no harm!"

"Y're evil, is why," said the old man called Laslo, his eyes glittering. "Enemies of the Great One. An' we been chosen t' help defeat his enemies."

"Who is this Great One?" Finn demanded.

One of the others stepped forward, the haft of his spear raised. "Y' want I sh'd thump him, Laslo?"

The old man waved him back, his eyes fixed on Finn. "The Great One, boy, is the Maker of All. An' the Destroyer, if he wants. He sent his messengers from the sky, t' cleanse the earth of evil. An' he chose us t' serve him, an' t' serve his messengers."

"I don't know what you're talking about," Finn said angrily.

"Other folks never do," the old man rasped. "'Cause they're *evil*, like they always was. Which is why the Great One sent his messengers, like a scourge, t' cleanse an' punish. Jus' as you'll be punished, boy, when The Claw comes."

"And who's The Claw?" Finn wanted to know. "Another messenger?"

"Y'll know that, soon enough," the old man said. He turned away, as if tiring of the conversation. "Right, boys, pick 'em up. An' y' c'n clout him if he gives any trouble."

Several hands grasped Finn and dumped him roughly on to a

16

crude stretcher, leather straps tied between the hafts of two spears. Baer was hoisted on to another stretcher, and through his anger Finn felt a surge of worry. The big Bloodkin was still unconscious, breathing hoarsely, as if serious damage had been done by that crushing blow to his head. But there was nothing Finn could do, except lie helpless and humiliated, as the robed men lifted the stretchers and set off at a brisk pace.

They travelled silently, except for old Laslo, who mumbled to himself in a half-audible sing-song chant. And they moved easily through the darkened landscape, as if their path was totally familiar to them. In less than two hours they entered a narrow pass, between two walls of rock. And soon the pass widened and deepened, becoming a mighty gorge that perhaps had been cut into the rock by some long-vanished mountain stream. The starlight was enough to show Finn that the gorge was a bleak, forbidding place – high, vertical cliffs on either side looming like prison walls above the flat, rock-strewn floor.

It seemed no less forbidding when, in the depths of the gorge, a larger group of people came to meet them, bearing torches that smoked and stank. Finn saw women and children among the group, all wearing the long shapeless robes, all as oddly pale as his captors. And then, as they moved farther along the gorge, Finn saw the reason for their pallor. In one precipitous cliff wall, he saw three rows of darkened openings that had to be the mouths of caves.

Each row of caves had a narrow ledge in front of it, running along the cliff walls. The first ledge, some fifteen metres above the gorge floor, had about eight caves opening off it. Roughly the same distance above, another ledge gave access to the second row of caves; and on the third level, another fifteen metres up, an even narrower ledge led to more caves. And some twenty metres above them, shadowily silhouetted against the stars, was the flat, sharp-edged summit of the cliff.

Tall, narrow ladders reached up, almost vertically, from ledge to ledge. They were crudely made from slender poles, the rungs bound on with rawhide, and looked flimsy and precarious. Yet the people ran up and down them with the speed and ease of long familiarity. They did not even find it too difficult to drag the bound forms of Finn and Baer up those trembling ladders to the third and topmost ledge.

There they were wordlessly dumped on to the dirt floor of an empty, reeking, lightless cave. From sounds beyond the cave mouth, Finn knew that his captors had descended again, and had also removed the ladder that reached up to that level. He also could tell that two of the men had remained, on the ledge outside the cave, as guards. These people were taking no chances, Finn thought. And offering none.

He wriggled up to a sitting position, leaning back against the rough stone wall of the cave. The roughness seemed peculiar – not a natural surface, but more as if the stone had been worked by crude tools. Had these people actually *carved out* the caves and ledges, from the cliffside? Or had they taken over caves carved by others, long before?

His mind fastened on to the question, as a distraction from discomfort and gnawing fear. Perhaps the caves had been made for some never-to-be-known reason back in the ancient past, which Finn's people called the Forgotten Time. He let his thoughts drift, musing, wondering . . .

All his life Finn had been filled with vague wonderings about what life had been like in the Forgotten Time. He knew, as most people did, that once human beings had ruled the entire world, thousands of millions of them. They had lived in great structures of stone and metal, served and protected by fantastic machines. And some of those machines were said to have been weapons of unimaginable power. In the end – no one knew why – the weapons were let loose, and somehow set the world on fire. The great structures were reduced to ash and rubble, and from all those millions of humans only a few thousand remained,

18

crawling half-dead among the ruins.

Yet those few survived. And over the years that followed – maybe hundreds of years – they began to recover. They might even have hoped to rebuild the world as it had been. But they did not have the chance.

With appalling suddenness, one day, the Forgotten Time had come to an end, and the world that Finn knew came into existence. A world of terror and death, of endless misery and inhuman cruelty.

On that one final and beginning day, the sky had abruptly been filled with immense and terrifying flying machines. The Earth's new masters had come, to impose their alien rule.

Finn had heard, many times, the story of the invasion of Earth. How the alien beings had emerged from the ships – tall, frightening humanoids, with spindly limbs and bulging torsos, small heads dominated by a slash of mouth and yellow rectangles of eyes. How they carried slim metal tubes that fired lethal rays of focused heat. How they used those weapons, coldly and almost casually, on any humans who ventured near.

And how even more powerful weapons were carried on the giant ships, as the humans learned to their cost. In a last desperate attempt to reclaim their world, the remnants of humanity tried to attack their invaders. But the aliens had merely used their ships in a systematic, ruthless eradication of humans, and what was left of their former civilization. For a second time the world went up in flames – and the few humans who survived that second holocaust fled in terror and despair to the wilderness that had already begun to spread itself back over much of the ravaged land.

There the few survivors eked out a wretched life of primitive drudgery and deep-rooted fear. And, surprisingly, from then on the aliens mostly ignored them – just as humans, in the days of their greatness, had mostly ignored the little creatures that scuttled in the corners of their civilization. In turn the humans tried to ignore the aliens. They had learned that there was to be no communication, no hope of understanding the invaders' effortlessly superior and coldly murderous ways. The humans merely hoped to be left alone.

But even there they hoped in vain.

The aliens sent out their batlike spywings on random inspections of the crude, scattered human villages. No village was allowed to grow too large, or to re-introduce any but the most basic forms of technology. If those unwritten rules were broken, aliens would arrive – in large, egg-shaped machines, hovering slightly above the ground on cushions of strange forces. Then the heat-rays would flash their deadly crimson, and humans would die.

But sometimes the aliens would come when no rules had been broken. And from those times, humanity at last found a name for their cruel, aloof, unfathomable masters. For on such visits some humans would be ruthlessly taken away, into captivity. Rumours said that some became beasts of burden at alien bases scattered across the land. Others, it was whispered, were used in mysterious, grisly experiments in alien laboratories. And none of those taken was ever seen again by their families and neighbours.

So humanity gave a name to the alien beings who had captured the Earth. They called them – the Slavers.

3

Sunrise Ceremony

FINN SHIFTED UNEASILY against the cave wall, as his mind dredged up the chill images of the past. There had been a time when tales of the coming of the Slavers had filled his curious young mind with more questions than answers. But in the recent, danger-filled months of his life, some of those questions had been answered. . . .

As a child, Finn had heard about the enslavement of Earth from the man he called father – Joshua Ferral, formerly the huntsman for the isolated forest village where Finn had grown up. But Finn knew that Josh was not his real father. He knew that Josh had found him in the forest – no more than a toddler, naked and alone but blithely unharmed in the midst of the wilderness. Josh had taken the child home, where he and his wife had named him Finn and had raised him as their own.

And in all the years of his growing up, where he had come from had remained a mystery. Josh had thought there might be a clue in a strange pattern of raised dark dots on Finn's upper left arm – but that, too, remained a mystery.

Still, Finn's childhood had been as happy as it could be within a huddled village in an enslaved world. He learned from Josh the arts and secrets of the wilderness – learned them with astonishing ease and speed, as if somehow he *belonged* to the wilds, as much at home there as a young lynx or hawk. In time Finn took over the role of village huntsman, so that the ageing

Josh, now a widower, could stay at home with his natural daughter, Jena, six years Finn's junior.

So the peaceful years had gone on. But as Finn grew towards young manhood, the shadow of fear that lay across the mind of every human was a constant reminder that, in that world, happiness could not be guaranteed to last. As it proved, for the Ferral family.

Without warning, Slavers had come to the village. When they left, they had taken new human slaves away with them. And two of those taken had been old Josh and Jena.

Other humans would have reacted with grief and mourning, with horror and bleak despair. But though Finn had felt all those things, he was not an ordinary human. He had set out – suicidally, the villagers warned – to try to rescue his loved ones.

His supreme wilderness skills enabled him to track even the 'whirlsleds', as the strange hovering machines were called. Eventually he found his way to a small Slaver base, where he first encountered the savage beast-men whom the aliens used to control their human slaves. In a night of high risk and wild violence – and a great deal of luck – Finn had wrecked the base and made his escape. But though he had learned much about the Earth's alien masters, and their bestial followers, he had not found Josh and Jena.

Then his pursuit led him westwards, and on the way he had come upon Baer, the renegade. Baer had been raised in a huge Slaver centre, far away in the western mountains, but since his escape he had been roaming the wilds, waging a single-handed war against the Slavers, and against his own kind, the Bloodkin. He and Finn joined forces, and from Baer Finn learned much – about the Slavers' cold, unimaginative ways, and about what uses they made of their human slaves.

Finn learned with horror that the Slavers forced their captives to mate, and then conducted experiments on the unborn embryos. They were somehow trying to change the biological nature of the human race. From those experiments the Bloodkin were the usual result, half-beasts born to slave women.

But Finn learned more when he and Baer risked their lives to penetrate another, larger Slaver base. There Finn found old Josh among the brutalized human slaves – and he and Baer led them in a grim and bloody battle for freedom. But before then, in the heart of the alien base, Finn had come upon the crushing truth of his own origin.

He had found the corpses of new-born human babies, not Bloodkin. He knew from Baer that normal babies were usually not born alive from the Slaver experiments. But in a mind-blasting realization Finn knew that at least one child, born that way, *had* survived. And he was that child.

For each of the tiny corpses that he had seen in the Slaver base had a pattern of raised dark dots on its upper left arm.

The knowledge had nearly destroyed him, until Baer later explained. The Slavers, he told Finn, were trying to erase what there was in humans that made them human – trying to turn evolution back, to make humans into docile, domesticated *animals*. Usually the experiments bred only the beast-like Bloodkin. Finn must have been a rare success – except that the alien experimenters had failed to erase his mind and his humanity. Instead, perhaps without knowing it, they had put *into* him all the instincts and natural abilities of a wilderness creature.

It was the same kind of accident that had bred into Baer more humanity than was found in other Bloodkin. Unwittingly, two special individuals had been created *by* the Slavers – to become the most dangerous enemies *of* the Slavers.

Finn was no longer troubled by the truth about his origin. Just as he was not troubled by the likelihood that the Slavers would try to pursue Baer and himself from then on. In that alien base the Slavers too had learned the truth about Finn. He knew that they would want to find out why and how he had survived, as much as they would want to crush the flame of human resistance that he represented. But Finn was more concerned with his long, arduous journey into the far west of the immense land.

After the escape from the Slaver base, old Josh had confirmed that, when he had been separated from Jena, the girl had been taken away in a whirlsled heading west. Finn had wondered if she might be taken to the vast Slaver city in the western mountains. There, according to Baer, the aliens carried out their most extensive experiments on humans, and were always in need of new slaves. And so there Finn was intending to go, to seek his foster sister – even though he knew that she might be elsewhere, or that she might not have survived the journey, and what awaited her at the journey's end . . .

In the empty blackness of the cave, Finn pushed that chilling thought away, and the panicky desperation that came with it. Whether Jena was alive or not might soon be of no more concern to him. Not if he remained, trussed like a turkey, waiting for traitorous humans to hand him over to some servant of the Slavers called The Claw.

His body threshed as he struggled for a moment against his bonds, and tears of frustration and fury stung his eyes as he knew that his struggles were useless. But in that moment, he heard the most welcome sound that he could imagine.

From the other side of the lightless cave, a rich bass rumble. "Finn? That you?"

"Baer!" Finn managed just in time to stifle his glad cry into a whisper. "Keep your voice down. We're in a cave on a cliffside, with two guards outside."

"An' we're tied up," Baer growled softly, "an' I got the grandaddy of all headaches. Tell me what's happenin'."

Quickly, in an undertone, Finn told him how they had been captured, and described the strangeness of their captors. Baer snarled softly at the thought of humans serving the Slavers –

and growled again, with an edge of anxiety, when Finn added that the humans were waiting for someone called The Claw.

"If The Claw's after us," Baer said, "we're in trouble."

"I'd kind of noticed that," Finn replied dryly. "Who is he?"

"I never set eyes on him," Baer said, "but I heard lots about him. Some say he's a Bloodkin, some say different. Gets his name from havin' a hand outa shape – fingers all grown together an' curved, like a hook. They say it's the only weapon he uses – an' the only one he needs."

Finn shivered slightly. "Why should he be after us?"

"'Cause that's what he does," Baer said. "Goes after people. He's a hunter, maybe near as good as you. But he hunts folks – for the Slavers. If a Bloodkin decides to quit servin' the *Masters* – " Baer nearly spat the word – "The Claw gets sent after him. He gets sent after just about anythin', or anyone, that's important to the Slavers."

"Like us," Finn said.

"Like us," Baer agreed. "After what we did back east, an' after the Slavers found out where you came from, I shoulda figured The Claw'd come huntin'. An' they say what The Claw goes to catch, gets caught."

"Again like us," Finn said bitterly.

Before Baer could reply, a noise from outside the cave distracted them. Turning his head, Finn saw the cave mouth outlined in a glimmer of light, chill and grey. The light of dawn, filtering slowly into the gorge's gloomy depths. And the noise from outside was the sound of a ladder being raised, and men ascending it.

"Finn," Baer hissed quickly, "make like I'm still out. Far's you know, I'm dyin'."

Finn nodded, then went still as the light at the cave mouth altered to orange, and four men entered, two with torches. One of the other two was old Laslo, who walked over and peered down at Baer. As before, Baer's eyes were closed, and he was breathing raggedly.

25

Laslo glanced at Finn. "He wake up at all?"

Finn shook his head, putting anxiety into his voice. "I think he's dying."

"Reckon we mashed his brains some," Laslo said, unperturbed. "Don't matter. It's you The Claw wants most." He turned to the other man. "One of you get the kid some food an' water. We got sun-up soon, an' The Claw'll be along any time."

One of the guards hurried out, returning in a few moments with two crude clay bowls, one containing water and the other holding some nameless brown sludge. Finn made no move towards them.

"He ain't hungry, Laslo," the guard snickered.

The old man shrugged. "He c'n eat or not, as he's a mind to. Won't be our concern much longer. Let's go, now. Sun-up any minute."

They moved towards the cave entrance, and for the first time Finn saw, with a surge of anger, that Laslo was wearing Baer's machete strapped round his waist, flapping against the folds of his grimy robe. Outside the cave, the group halted on the ledge, and simply stood there, still and silent, as if waiting. Around them Finn watched the daylight brightening – and then saw a streak of gold as the rising sun lifted itself above the clifftop, and flung the first of its rays down into the dank shadows of the gorge.

At that moment, Laslo raised his arms high. When he spoke, his normal rasping voice had risen into a high, chanting tone that was picked up and amplified by echoes from the vast stone cliffs.

"People of the Gorge!"

From below, Finn could hear a vague, breathy murmur, as if all the cave-dwelling people had gathered on the floor of the gorge. It was a ceremony, he realized – some kind of ritual for the sunrise.

"People of the Gorge!" Laslo repeated. "Give praise to the

Great One Beyond! The Great One who guards our days, who blesses us with peace and safety, who has marked us to be his Chosen! The Great One who sent the mightiest of his servants to purge the world with flame, to burn out the evil in the hearts of men! Praise him!"

"Praise the Great One," replied the people, in a ragged sonorous chorus.

"We, the Chosen," intoned the old man, "who await our Day of Emergence into the green lands of plenty, are blessed with the joy of serving the messengers of the Great One. At their bidding, we seek out evil and cleanse it, as we have cleansed evil from ourselves. At their bidding, we sought two evildoers among the mountains. We overcame them, and bound them, and they are here."

"Praise the One," breathed the people.

"Soon the servants of the Great One will come," Laslo continued, "and the evildoers will receive their punishment. Just as we will receive our reward, both here and in the Day of Emergence to come! Praise the Great One!"

"Praise him!" shouted the people rapturously. "Praise him!"

Laslo might well have gone on in similar vein, but at that moment the ceremony was interrupted. Above the fading echoes of the people's cry, another sound intruded into the gorge. A sound that Finn knew well, that lifted the hair on the back of his neck and sent icy fear sweeping through him.

The ominous, throbbing hum of a Slaver whirlsled.

4

Cave of Death

AS THE SOUND of the alien machine grew, Laslo lowered his arms and hurried out of view, rapidly followed by the others. Finn listened to their swift descent, and knew that two of them had stayed behind on the ledge, as before, to guard the cave.

"That'll be The Claw," Baer rumbled softly.

"In a whirlsled?" Finn whispered, surprised. Baer had told him that the Slavers almost never taught their Bloodkin servants how to use their machines.

"Seems so." Baer's nod was clearly visible as the light strengthened within the cave. "Looks like The Claw is a kinda special Bloodkin – or not Bloodkin at all."

"Then what is he?" Finn asked.

Baer shrugged, then paused. From the depths of the gorge they heard a flurry of voices, followed again by the noise of feet on a ladder – some rising rapidly, others climbing more slowly.

"I figure we're gonna find out," Baer said at last. "Remember – I'm dyin'."

He closed his eyes and resumed his heavy, ragged breathing a second before Laslo burst back into the cave, accompanied by two men who were probably the guards from outside.

"Praise the One, praise the One." Laslo's eyes were glittering feverishly. "The day of deliverance is at hand."

"Praise him," the guards echoed dutifully, glancing back towards the cave mouth. Finn twisted to look in the same direction, in time to see the hulking forms of three Bloodkin shoulder through the entrance.

Finn had seen one of them before – the one he had left unconscious back in the mountains. He was recognisable from the discoloured lump jutting between his eyebrows, and from the venomous glare that he flung at Finn. But Finn hardly noticed. His attention was fixed on the last figure to appear in the cave mouth.

The figure was tall and powerfully built, but moving with the lean suppleness of an athlete, boots silent on the dirt floor. He wore a dark-coloured garment, like a close-fitting coverall, which eerily resembled the strange dark covering on the body of a Slaver. But the newcomer was no alien – nor was he a Bloodkin. His face was a human face. Chiselled cheekbones, a thin, cruel mouth, and a domed, sculpted head that was entirely hairless.

Finn took in all those details in one glance, before his gaze settled on the newcomer's left hand. The fingers of that hand were not separated, and were curled inwards slightly, like a tapering extension of the muscular palm. And the fingernails were also bonded together, so that fingers and nails formed a single growth, with the density and toughness of horn – a curved and monstrous talon.

With Laslo hovering at his side, the stranger who was surely The Claw stepped forward to gaze down at Finn, his eyes lingering for a moment on the pattern of dark dots on Finn's upper left arm. And Finn, in turn, was staring with chill horror at The Claw's bare left arm – which bore a similar pattern.

"You are very young to have so troubled the Masters." The Claw's voice was flat and cold as a winter graveyard. "What are you called?"

"Finn Ferral." Finn's voice was also flat, and as calm as he could manage.

The Claw let his eyes drift again across the marks on Finn's arm. "It seems we are two of a kind, Finn Ferral."

Finn glared. "I'm my own kind. There's no likeness between us."

"But there is," the cold voice said. "Your skills in the wild are said to be nearly the equal of mine. And I know that you are uncommonly hard to track, even for me. No, we are much alike. There are no others like us among the creations of the Masters."

With that The Claw turned away, indifferent to Finn's glower, and stood over the motionless form of Baer. "And the renegade, whose desertion was oddly never reported. I am told he is dying. But I am sure that you, Finn Ferral, will be able to answer my questions about him."

Finn recalled that Baer had been believed dead by the other Bloodkin of the mountain city where he had lived. No one had suspected that he had survived, so no one had reported him as a runaway.

The Claw bent slightly. Then, without warning, he struck downwards with his monstrous left hand, a blow so swift that even Finn's eyes could barely follow it. The sharp tip of that fearsome talon sliced neatly across Baer's broad chest, leaving a thin line of red amid the hair.

But not a muscle of Baer's body twitched, even slightly. Nor did the ragged breathing alter.

Finn had jerked and gasped at the blow, as if his own body had been slashed. But when Baer remained immobile he sank back, relieved. Baer must have had an eye slitted open, imperceptibly, to guard against just such a test of his unconsciousness.

"No doubt he is in a coma," The Claw said coldly. "But I will take them both. If the renegade dies on the way, it is no matter."

"As y' say, excellence," Laslo fawned.

"Two of my men will remain with you, to make room in the sled," The Claw went on, indicating the Bloodkin. "We will rest with you today, and begin our return journey this evening. You have done well, Laslo."

30

"Thank y', excellence," Laslo burbled, his head bobbing. "Praise the One."

"Indeed." The cold voice was as emotionless as stone. "And your reward will follow. When I return again, I will lead you to the land that has been promised you, once we have . . . *cleansed* it, as you would say."

"Praise the Great One!" Laslo babbled, his eyes glittering.

Finn could contain himself no longer. "How can you do this?" he exploded. "You're *human*!"

"Am I?" The Claw gazed emptily at Finn, slightly lifting his terrible left hand. "Most humans – aside from the People of the Gorge – are the vermin of this world, cowering through lives of darkness and terror. I am not of them. I am the beginning of a new race. A race that you could have been part of, Finn Ferral, had you not chosen to join the vermin."

He turned and strode out of the cave, with the others crowding hastily after.

Across from Finn Baer stirred. "Nice fella," he growled. "Lotsa personal charm."

"Are you all right?" Finn asked quickly.

"Sure. Just nicked the skin. An' I was ready for it." Baer grunted softly as he heaved his massive strength against the unyielding rawhide. "Anyways, now we got all day to work on gettin' outa here."

"Out?" Finn stared. "Tied up like this, and stuck on this cliff?"

"You don't wanta give up so easy, young Finn," Baer rumbled. "We're not beat till we're dead. Let's just keep our heads an' do some figurin', an' see what we come up with."

Many long hours later, as the slow day drew to its end and the light within the cave began to fade, Finn and Baer were sitting exactly as they had been, arms and legs still encased in the wrappings of rawhide thongs. But in fact they were no longer bound. Throughout those tedious hours, Baer's powerful teeth had gnawed tirelessly at Finn's bonds, until at last his arms were free. And then it had been his turn, slowly and patiently, to work on the bulky knots in the remaining thongs, until finally both of them were loose. Baer had then taken a moment to gulp the water and the foul, sludgy bowl of food that had been brought for Finn, while the two of them pondered the possibilities. In the end they had come up with a plan of action. It was crazily risky, and full of flaws, as they both knew – but they also knew it was their only chance.

So they had twined the rawhide things loosely around their arms and legs again, to look as securely bound as before, and settled down to wait. And now twilight was entering the gorge, and the waiting would soon be over.

"Just as long as they don't *all* come again," Finn whispered.

"I figure it'll just be the people," Baer replied. "The Bloodkin won't be up to carryin' us down the ladders. An' The Claw's the boss, so he'd never come get us himself."

Finn looked dubious, but he did not get a chance to reply. From outside came the now-familiar sound of a ladder being raised to the ledge, followed by the clatter of climbing feet.

Several men crowded into the deepening gloom of the cave, and Finn breathed silent thanks. Baer had guessed correctly. They were all humans – five of the robed men with spears, and old Laslo behind them, Baer's machete still flapping round his legs.

Laslo gestured at two of the men, who moved towards Finn, while he and the other three gathered beside Baer.

"I think he's dead," Finn said.

Baer's eyes were half-open, with only the whites showing, and there was no sign of breathing. "Looks like it," Laslo nodded. "But The Claw wants him anyway. Let's go."

The two men next to Finn bent over him, one reaching for his shoulders while the other stooped to grasp his feet. But his hands never took a grip.

The broken rawhide thongs fell away as Finn's feet lashed upwards. The savage kick drove all the breath from the man's body, and flung him backwards to crash into Laslo and the other three men. All five of them fell in a tangled, threshing heap, on top of Baer.

By then Finn was on his feet, confronting the man who had reached for his shoulders. Furiously, the man slashed with his spear at Finn's head. But Finn dodged the blow, catlike – and then, as the man stumbled, off balance, Finn sprang at his throat.

The fury of the attack drove the man backwards, to collide with the wall of the cave. His head struck the rock with a sodden thump, and he went limp, sliding as if boneless from Finn's grasp.

Finn whirled towards the sounds of battle across the cave, in time to see that Baer had surged up from beneath the tangled heap of five humans. One of Baer's great hands gripped the skinny throat of Laslo, while the other hand held the machete, plucked from Laslo's belt. At Baer's feet, two robed bodies lay crumpled and bleeding. And in the instant that Finn turned, the machete drove like a skewer into the heart of another man.

But the last man, Finn saw with horror, was in full flight for the mouth of the cave. Three more strides and he would have been out – screaming a warning to The Claw.

He took only one and a half of those strides. Finn swept up the spear that had been dropped by the man he had felled, and flung it with all his deadly accuracy. The barbed head drove into the fleeing man's back, and dropped him in a lifeless sprawl at the very edge of the cave mouth.

"Good throw," Baer said casually. "Coulda got lively if he fell over the ledge."

By then old Laslo had joined the other still figures on the floor, his neck twisted awry, and Baer was calmly strapping the machete on to his back. For a moment Finn felt that he was going to be sick. He had killed Slavers and Bloodkin, but never humans. And however traitorous the People of the Gorge were, they were still human.

Baer peered at him anxiously. "Let's get goin', 'fore the others start wonderin'," he urged. "An' you could take the knife off that fella."

He was pointing to the sizeable dagger in the belt of the man whose head had so crushingly struck the wall. Finn swallowed heavily, and reached for the weapon. It fitted his empty sheath well enough, but it did not make him any happier.

"Let's *go*," Baer repeated, urgently.

Finn nodded, and moved noiselessly out of the cave, crouching, invisible in the gathering darkness. The ledge was deserted, so the usual guards were no doubt among the dead in the cave. Flat on his belly, he peered carefully over the lip of the ledge. On the floor of the gorge a small crowd of people milled, some of them bearing torches. The light gleamed on the metallic, egg-shaped bulk of the whirlsled, standing silent nearby, and on the hairless domed head of The Claw, waiting impassively with his Bloodkin next to the machine.

Finn sighed with relief. Whatever noise had been made during that savage fight had been contained within the cave. Even The Claw suspected nothing. But he soon would, Finn knew, when Laslo and the others did not reappear.

The thought shook him out of his dejection. Silently he drifted along the ledge, towards the top of the ladder that Laslo's men had used. Slowly, delicately, hand over hand, he began to pull it up.

Then his heart almost stopped. Below him, he had seen The Claw stir, and say something to the three Bloodkin. And they began ambling away, one carrying a torch, towards the nearest ladder that led up to the lowest of the cliffside ledges.

The Claw had sent his men to hurry Laslo up. Which meant that time had run out for Finn and Baer.

But by then Finn had his ladder up, propped on the ledge, reaching up into the blackness towards the top of the cliff above. It stood almost vertically – and Baer, cautiously joining Finn on the narrow ledge, stared up uneasily.

"How'm I gonna climb that?" he rumbled.

"Now who's giving up too easily?" Finn whispered. "I'll go first, and hold the top somehow, to keep it steady. But we have to be quick!"

They both glanced down. The three Bloodkin were climbing slowly, as wary of the ladders as Baer was. But they had already reached the first and lowest of the ledges.

Finn turned and sprang up the ladder like a frightened squirrel. But then his heart sank. From the ledge he had not seen, in the darkness, how far upwards the ladder reached. Now, at the top of the ladder, he found that it was too short. Some five metres of vertical rock remained, up to the lip of the cliff.

Still, he realized, the sheer rock was deeply scarred and pitted, and he knew that he could climb it with ease. But – could Baer?

He looked down, and saw then that, whatever happened, there was no going back. A faint orange glow was reaching up to the ledge where Baer waited. And with it came a sudden burst of growling yells. The three Bloodkin had reached the second ledge, and had seen in the light of their torch the shadowy shapes of the escaping prisoners.

"Come up fast!" Finn shouted to Baer, careless now of noise.

The ladder trembled as Baer's weight came on to it. After endless moments, he had neared the top, where Finn perched.

"Didn't work out, did it?" he growled sourly, looking up at the sheer wall of rock.

But a desperate idea had leaped into Finn's mind. "Go on past me!" he hissed. "I'll guide you!"

As he spoke, he was reaching for handholds to his left, edging *sideways* – off the ladder, clinging like a fly to the rock face.

Baer did not stop to argue. The rising light of the Bloodkin torch, below, helped him, and so did Finn's non-stop directions. "Left hand up – higher – there – now the right hand – over a bit – jam your foot in that crack . . . "

So it went, with tortuous slowness. But Baer's immense strength dragged him upwards, and it was in reality only moments before he was heaving his shaggy bulk over the crest of the cliff.

Yet by then the three Bloodkin had reached the topmost ledge and were swarming up the ladder in Baer's wake, knives and fangs gleaming in the torchlight.

Clamping his aching fingers on to their holds, Finn thrust out a leg towards the nearest of the ladder's uprights. The toe of his boot hooked behind the slim pole, and he took a deep breath, oblivious to the raging snarls of the Bloodkin only a few rungs below. But those snarls turned to howls of terror as Finn braced himself, and then, with all his strength, kicked his foot outwards, away from the rock wall.

The ladder had been nearly vertical to begin with, which gave him the leverage he needed. Finn's kick sent it swaying backwards, seeming to hesitate for a breathless instant, then toppling away and down like a felled tree. And with it fell the three Bloodkin, screaming in that long plunge to the floor of the gorge.

The cliffs were still echoing with those screams as Finn clawed his way up the rock face, to be dragged over the lip of the cliff by Baer's powerful hands. They rose to their feet together, looking down for the last time. And from the depths below them, another cry rose to resound between those sheer walls.

The voice of The Claw, raised in a savage, maniacal scream of raw fury – the scream of a predator whose prey has escaped it.

PART TWO

Riders of the Wastes

5

Oasis

THEY STOOD ON a low, rocky promontory, gazing out over the expanse of land that stretched before them to a distant horizon, shimmering with heat waves. The mid-afternoon sun struck down pitilessly, a golden fury in a sky bleached almost white by the glare. The high, brush-covered reaches of the mountains lay behind them now, as they moved into open country – like a gigantic, shallow basin, stretching bleak, dry and forbidding as far as the eye could see.

"Hot," Finn said idly.

Baer nodded. "Hot an' nasty. An' it'll get nastier, the deeper we go."

"Could be worse," Finn replied. He had always expected the Wasteland to be a vast, flat, featureless plain. But here the land was humped up into dunes and mounds, rocky ridges and knolls, tall mesas and jutting hills. Between those different kinds of heights there were stretches of flat, dusty earth – but there were also low-lying dips and hollows and depressions, just as rock-strewn as the hills. So there would be some cover, Finn saw, to shelter them from eyes in the sky.

"This's just the edge of the Wasteland," Baer was saying. "An' there's still lotsa ways to get dead, even here."

"So the middle of it is worse?" Finn asked.

"That's what I've heard. Special kinds of nastiness, an' critturs outa nightmares. When I came this way I kept to the

38

edges, an' even then I nearly didn't make it. Even Slavers sometimes don't make it."

"But Slavers *do* come this way?"

"Sure," Baer said. "But they travel in straight lines – you know that. An' their main route keeps 'em away from the middle."

"Then we'll have to watch out for them," Finn said lightly.

"Son, out here you hafta watch out for *everythin*'."

"Including people?"

Baer snorted. "Don't get on that again. If there's people peculiar enough to live in the Wasteland, which I doubt, I don't wanta meet 'em. Prob'ly be worse'n the People of the Gorge."

Finn smiled. It was a long-standing disagreement. Back in the eastern forest, after he and Baer had freed the humans from the Slaver base, those people had decided to travel west to seek a new home. Their leader, scar-faced Gratton, had heard that the Wasteland offered a refuge for humans, where Slavers would not pursue them. Baer had scoffed at the idea – but Finn had wanted it to be true.

Because old Josh, his foster father, was with that group – travelling more slowly, no doubt confronting their own obstacles and dangers. Finn fretted constantly about having to leave Josh, but he and the old man had agreed that the search for Jena had to come first. And now only the barrier of the Wasteland lay between Finn and the western mountains where his search might end.

"Let's be on our way," he said.

Baer nodded, and set off down the slope. Finn glanced up at the pale sky, and followed. It was a pattern they had maintained ever since they had fled from the gorge. Finn had no doubt about The Claw's skill in the wilderness: he had certainly located them in the mountains, and put the People of the Gorge on their trail. And he would just as certainly be tracking them now. In fact Finn had expected him to come up the cliffside of the gorge, on their heels – but it had been only a mob of the robed humans who had come screaming up the ladders after them, and it had been easy to elude their blundering search. Baer had guessed that The Claw would not abandon his whirlsled, so he would have to come the long way around to the clifftop to pick up their trail. But he would pick it up. So, from then on, Baer had led, while Finn followed, using every scrap of his own skill to obliterate their trail.

It had slowed their pace, but to make up for it they had travelled night and day, snatching only brief catnaps. Finn had made a new sling from leather strips cut from his jerkin, but he spared little time for hunting and less for eating. And so they had covered an enormous amount of ground, in that almost non-stop flight, and had seen no signs of pursuit.

But Baer did not find that hopeful. "The Claw won't quit," he had said. "He'll know which way we're goin' – an' he might be circlin' round ahead of us, settin' traps."

"Like he did in the mountains," Finn had said.

"Yep," Baer had grinned. "An' he got us, there."

"He won't get us again," Finn had snarled.

"Maybe he won't hafta," Baer had said. "He could just let the Wasteland get us."

After two days of travel into the sun-baked desolation, Finn knew what Baer meant. Only once or twice had they seen anything like vegetation, and that had been merely a few clumps of thorny scrub that looked dead. The Wasteland was waterless, lifeless and merciless. And Finn was worried. Their flight from the mountains had drained their energies – and now, after those two days in the Wasteland, they had no food and only a few mouthfuls left in Baer's water-bottle.

"There's got to be water somewhere, even out here," he said to Baer at last, his voice a dry croak.

"Sure." Even Baer's rich bass sounded dust-choked. "But it's a big place."

"I noticed," Finn said wryly. He halted, and ahead of him Baer stopped as well, great shoulders sagging wearily in the relentless heat. They were moving through one of the low hollows, where the sloping sides held bare outcroppings of rock that would not show their tracks. Finn turned and plodded to the top of the slope, gazing at the terrain around.

The landscape seemed unending, and unchanging. Dunes and ridges and hollows, and now and then a high tower or spire of rock carved by wind and weather into an eerie, distorted sculpture. The hot breath of the wind flung dust towards him, and he felt it grating against his red-rimmed eyes, tasted its alkaline bitterness in his parched mouth.

"If you see a lake of cool blue water," Baer said gloomily, "it's a mirage."

"No lakes," Finn replied absently. Just rock and sand, he thought to himself, marching on and on. And nothing moving on it, except whirls of dust lifted by the wind, and heat-waves dancing on every part of the horizon. . . .

Almost every part.

He strained his aching eyes to their utmost. One small area in the remote distance did not seem the same as the rest of the land. It seemed to have an odd smudginess, a different texture. It lay to the south, away from their westward line of travel – but some instinct drew Finn towards it.

"Let's swing south a while," he said to Baer. "There's something I want to look at."

"That figures," Baer sighed. "While we die of thirst, we can do a little sightseein'."

But he turned southwards, having learned to respect Finn's instincts. And after more kilometres of weary trudging, Finn had the proof that his hunch was right. The wind shifted, again bringing dust into their faces, but bringing something else as well – something that made Finn lift his head, sniffing, his eyes lighting up.

"That's water! Smell it?"

"All I smell is dust," Baer rumbled. But his eyes brightened, too, as they quickened their pace. And in a few minutes they slid over the sandy brink of a low hill and saw the promise of survival spread before them.

It was a shallow depression, at least half a kilometre across. And it was thick with vegetation – much of it tall and richly foliaged. That was what Finn had seen, as an indistinct smudge in the distance. And the sight gladdened the heart of the forest creature Finn would always be.

But the gladness faded a little, as they drew nearer. There was a *wrongness* about every plant, every leaf and branch.

Some of the plants were swollen and bulbous, some were skinny as bones. Some bore clumps of moss-like hair instead of leaves, others were all broad, flat leaves without stems. There were squat plants like a madman's idea of a cactus, and high trees whose every surface centimetre bristled with thorns. And winding, entangling through them all was a profusion of creepers and vines in various sickly shades of brown and green.

They entered the brush warily, and Finn soon saw that it held animal life, too, mostly with the same wrongness. He saw a mockery of a snake, with an outsized head and skin as bumpy and gnarled as ancient stone. He saw things like lizards, but in place of skin they had only a coating of viscous slime. He saw insects, of sorts, most of them unsettlingly large, many of them with too many legs, covered in dark fur or thick, ridged shell.

"If there's water here," Finn said wonderingly, "it'll probably poison us."

"Could be," Baer grunted. "That's the Wasteland way."

But again his pessimism proved wrong. The weird oasis held a small, clear pool at its centre, fed from an underground spring – and when Finn worked up the courage to take a small, wary sip, he found it brackish but drinkable. Despite the taste, it was nectar in their dust-dry mouths.

As Baer refilled the water-bottle, Finn was unwrapping his sling. "I'll go see if there's anything that looks edible."

"Hope there is," Baer said, stretching hugely. "I'm hungrier'n I am tired – an' I'm dam' tired."

"Then rest a while," Finn smiled. "Maybe back where we came into this place – so you can keep an eye on our back trail."

"Right," Baer nodded. "An' you . . . "

But as so often before, he found he was talking to himself. Finn had stepped into the tangle of greenery, and disappeared. Shaking his head, Baer turned away, towards the edge of the oasis, looking for a comfortable place to sit.

Finn by then was moving in the opposite direction, across the oasis. But it was not until he had reached the far side, where some low thorn bushes led out into open terrain again, that he saw something worth pursuing. A snake, seeming slightly odd, for it had a growth on its tail that buzzed when Finn drew near. But otherwise it looked as a snake should look, and had none of the *wrongness* about it that Finn had instinctively felt in the other creatures. As the snake slid away, Finn silently followed, sling ready.

But then he halted. His uncanny hearing had picked up the ghost of a sound, like a steady pounding or drumming. He could even feel the vibrations of it, faintly, in the ground. He crept forward, crouching among the sparse thorn-bushes, staring out at the dusty land beyond the oasis. And as he stared, up over a ridge nearly a kilometre away, swept a large, swirling cloud of dust.

The drumming sound, he realized, was coming from the dust-cloud – at least, from the shapes vaguely visible within the cloud. Tall shapes, yet strangely elongated, and travelling at speed . . .

Horsemen.

They were not heading for the oasis, Finn saw, but their course would bring them near enough for him to see if they were humans – or something else. He shifted position slightly, to improve his view. And as he moved, a menacing buzz sounded almost beneath his feet.

43

It was just enough warning. He leaped, high and sideways, like a startled cat, as the fanged head of the snake flashed in a blur through the place where his leg had been.

But the reflexive leap exposed him. The dust-cloud slowed – then increased its speed again, swinging ominously towards the oasis.

Finn whirled and fled back to the denser brush, then paused and looked back. The horsemen had swiftly come up to the edge of the outlying thornbushes, and were leaping down from their mounts in an explosion of dust. Nine of them – though one stayed with the horses while the other eight began to move cautiously towards the oasis.

And they *were* human. But they were like no humans Finn had ever seen. They wore only wrappings of cloth at their loins, and knee-high boots of soft leather. Their skin was a coppery brown, and their hair was long and black, held back by strips of bright cloth round their heads. Most of them seemed to have patches of discoloured skin, bright red or yellow or white, on their faces and chests. But Finn was more aware of the fact that they were lean, muscular and supple, and that they were heavily armed – knives at their belts, short spears or bows and arrows in their hands.

Finn drew back, letting the greenery swallow him up. He had no reason to assume that these copper-skinned strangers were enemies – but his experience with the People of the Gorge made him unwilling to show himself. It would make more sense to find Baer and then hope they would remain hidden, until perhaps the strangers tired of the search. . . .

A sudden realization chopped off his thoughts. He himself was, as usual, creating not a whisper of sound as he moved. But there were eight men somewhere in the brush behind him.

And not even Finn's hearing could detect their movement.

He increased his pace nervously. Aside from old Josh, he had never known any humans who were so at home in the wilderness. And a chilling thought struck him. He had not looked at the strangers' left arms. Could they, too, be creations of the Slavers – like himself and The Claw?

But whatever they were, he thought grimly, they were too skilled: he and Baer could not hope to elude them within the confines of the oasis. Sooner or later, there would be a fight.

But when he drew near the other edge of the oasis, where Baer should be waiting, his heart seemed to stop beating, and the copper-skinned humans were almost forgotten.

There was no sign of Baer. Instead, there was a dark, bat-winged shape wheeling in the sky – and on the slope beyond the oasis there was another cloud of dust. A cloud that was settling, for what had caused it had come to a stop.

A whirlsled.

Finn felt frozen, despite the desert heat. Was this The Claw, more swift and deadly on their trail than he and Baer had dreamed?

The top of the whirlsled opened. But it was not The Claw that emerged.

It was two tall, narrow beings with spindly arms and legs, small heads on skinny necks, oddly bulging bodies with a dark covering more like skin than clothing.

Slavers – gripping in their three-clawed hands the dark metal tubes that were the lethal weapons called heatlances.

One of the aliens opened its slit of mouth and emitted a series of strangled, crackling sounds. The other replied, and both stared round at the edge of the brush with their rectangular yellow eyes. Finn crouched, unseen, not breathing, as the colour of those eyes shifted slightly to a lurid orange, and the two aliens began to stalk towards the oasis.

6

Rainshadow

FINN REMAINED STILL, close to panic at the thought of being trapped between two sets of enemies. But then his instincts took charge, and he vanished back into the undergrowth, desperately trying to work out what to do.

It was possible that the two Slavers and the group of strange humans might be allied somehow, perhaps in pursuit of Baer and himself. But if that was not true, the humans were also in danger. And something in Finn rebelled at the idea of letting any humans walk unsuspectingly into the heatlances of the aliens. There had to be a way. . . .

Then his muddled thoughts broke off. He had heard an almost inaudible sound, like a trill. It sounded like a signal – and it was unnervingly close to the tangle of green where Finn had instantly flattened himself. He raised his head silently, and glimpsed a copper-brown leg, only a few paces away.

Again instinct took over. As the owner of the leg moved past, barely stirring a leaf, Finn crept after him in an equally complete silence. As he did so, he drew the knife that he had brought from the gorge.

Now the stranger was directly ahead, a spear held lightly in one muscular hand. Swift as the snake that had nearly struck him, Finn flung his left arm forward, clamping his hand over the other man's mouth, as his right hand brought the knife up, its point pressed against the man's neck.

"*Don't move!*" Finn hissed. "Drop the spear!"

The stranger's body jerked in a spasm of shock, but Finn's steely grip held firm. Then the other man froze into stillness, letting the spear fall silently. Finn felt relief that the man understood his words – and part of his mind also felt admiration for the control, and courage, that kept the man from struggling.

"Now move ahead – slowly and quietly."

The man stepped carefully forward, silent despite his tension, and Finn moved with him, his grip not relaxing for an instant. Within a few paces the man halted, tensing even more. Through the veil of leaves and branches he had seen the two Slavers, still slowly advancing to the edge of the brush.

"Those *things*," Finn whispered, "are my enemies. Are they enemies to you?"

Without hesitation the man nodded, sharply.

"Then," Finn said, "we should not fight one another."

Aware of the huge risk he was taking, he released his grip and stepped back, knife ready. The stranger spun, staring. And Finn saw that he was not much older than himself – and that what had looked like discoloured skin on the bodies of the strangers was in fact paint. This one had a narrow stripe of white across both prominent cheekbones, matching the strip of white cloth round his head.

"No one has ever taken me by surprise like that," the stranger whispered, still staring at Finn with frank curiosity.

"We'll talk about it later," Finn said quickly. "The Slavers will be in the bush in a minute."

"I will gather my warriors," the man said, beginning to turn away.

"Wait!" Finn hissed. "I have a companion too. A Bloodkin –" he saw the stranger's eyes widen – "but one who fights the Slavers. Tell your men he's on our side."

The man studied Finn briefly, then nodded. "I will tell them."

He turned away to the greenery, and was gone. Finn blinked.

47

If their positions had been reversed, he wondered, could he have heard that one, creeping up behind?

But then he too was moving, back towards the edge of the oasis, desperately hoping that the stranger had been telling the truth about being an enemy of the Slavers. In a moment he could see the two aliens again, now standing at the fringe of the brush, peering into its depths. He slipped away to one side, thinking quickly. Slavers, he knew, were logical, predictable beings, lacking imagination, unable to make intuitive mental leaps or inspired guesses. That weakness had helped Finn before – and now he hoped to use it to split the pair up, and overcome them more easily.

Behind a bulky, cancerous-looking tree, he fitted a stone into his sling, took a deep breath, and shouted. "Baer!"

The call instantly attracted a burst of concentrated heat from both heatlances, as the aliens reacted to the sound. But the rays chewed harmlessly into the bulging tree-trunk.

"Over here!" came Baer's growling yell.

The heatlances swung, and the rays hissed through the greenery in the direction of Baer's voice. But Finn smiled, knowing that Baer too would have found ample protection.

"There're other humans in the bush!" he yelled. "They're on our side!" More heatrays sizzled past his tree.

"They better be!" roared Baer.

As the alien weapons again swung to seek Baer out, Finn peered past a cluster of leaves. The two aliens had begun to separate, each edging towards one of the two unseen voices from the brush. Their eyes now glittered a pale blue, like rectangles of ice. But out of either arrogance or lack of imagination, they were not seeking cover. They stood openly, weapons ready, waiting for a glimpse of the enemy.

Finn provided it. Sling whirling, he stepped out from behind the tree, released the stone, and leaped back. The two heatlances came sharply to bear on him – but neither fired.

Finn's stone struck with pinpoint accuracy into one of the

glaring eyes of the nearest Slaver. And at the same moment a storm of spears and arrows leaped from the brush. The copper-skinned strangers had entered the battle.

The nearest Slaver, already staggering with its crushed eye, fell in a sprawl of limbs, arrows lodged in its throat and other eye. More of the arrows had flashed upwards, to bring down the circling spywing. But the second Slaver remained unhurt. Some of the missiles had missed – and others had struck its bulky torso, bouncing away as if from armour. And the alien had wheeled and was raking the greenery with its murderous heatray.

Finn heard a choking cry from behind the foliage. But in the same moment, from another direction, a different weapon appeared – a spinning, glittering machete. Its razor edge sliced with deadly neatness across the Slaver's scrawny neck, and the alien corpse tumbled headless into the dust.

As Finn stepped out, Baer also emerged, grinning merrily, stopping to reclaim his machete. "Pretty good, eh?" Then Baer swung his great head towards the brush. "Where're these other . . . "

He did not complete the question. Instead, his mouth fell open as the copper-brown figures seemed to materialize, without sound, from the foliage.

"Dam', boy!" Baer breathed. "You been givin' them lessons in sneakin' round?"

Finn's mouth twitched, but he remained silent, watchful, as the young man with the white stripes on his face stepped forward. He too seemed watchful, especially as he eyed the huge bulk of Baer.

"We have fought together," the young man said solemnly to Finn, "and have slain our enemies."

Baer growled. "Thought for a minute you weren't gonna leave me any."

The stranger turned his level gaze on Baer. "You are the Bloodkin who fights for humans, against Slavers." It was a flat

49

statement, but it held a question.

"And against other Bloodkin," Finn put in. "He's my friend, a friend to humans."

The other man kept his gaze on Baer. "I have never known a Bloodkin to befriend humans."

Baer's bright eyes met his gaze firmly. "An' I never knew there was a buncha folks like you. So what? We just killed us a couple Slavers. That's what matters. I been killin' Slavers since prob'ly 'fore you were born. Anyone wants to join in, I'm on their side."

The stranger held the gaze for a moment, then calmly nodded. "Good." He switched his level stare to Finn. "You fought well. And you are our equal, or better, in the wilds. I have met no other white man like you."

"That's 'cause there aren't any," Baer said cheerfully. "Finn's more a wild crittur than a man. More 'n me, too, whatever I look like."

A ripple of amusement swept through the silently watching group of strangers, and Finn could feel the tension ease.

"I'm Finn Ferral," he said, "and this is Baer."

The other man nodded. "I am called. . . . " But the spatter of syllables meant nothing to Finn.

Baer, too, was frowning. "You got a nickname or somethin', that a fella can get his tongue round?"

The stranger smiled faintly. "In this language, my name would be Rainshadow."

"Real suitable, out in this desert," Baer said with a chuckle.

This time the smile broke out fully, a flash of white teeth against copper-brown. "It rains sometimes, even here. And it is a traditional name among my people."

"And who *are* your people?" Finn asked.

"We descend from those whom *your* people called Indians, in the Forgotten Time," Rainshadow said. "The first owners of this land, before the white man."

Finn and Baer looked puzzled, but impressed. "Are there

50

more of you?" Finn asked.

"Many hundreds in the Wasteland. And many whites among them, and others."

Baer grunted. "So the stories're right – there *are* folks here. I never woulda figured."

"Where did you all come from?" Finn asked.

"My people were always here, in the west," Rainshadow replied. "Those who survived the end of the Forgotten Time hid from the Slavers in the Wasteland. But now, today, we do not always hide."

There was a murmur of grim agreement among the other Indians, but Finn looked at them blankly. "What do you mean?"

"Slavers cross the Wasteland often," Rainshadow explained, "moving to or from their great mountain city. Often we attack them. Those two – " he gestured towards the dead aliens – "were coming from the mountains. We were riding to intercept them, when we saw you."

"You woulda jumped a whirlsled?" Baer said, amazed. "Just with spears an' things?"

Rainshadow smiled fiercely. "The Slavers are vulnerable in many ways, as I think you know."

But the subject had jolted Finn into noticing a fact that he had been only unconsciously aware of. "There are only seven of you here," he said. "But I saw eight before."

"A warrior was injured," Rainshadow said gravely. "He has returned to the horses to tend his wound."

Finn nodded. By then, a new thought had struck him – one that drove every other concern from his mind. "In your attacks on Slavers," he asked carefully, "do you ever . . . free any slaves?"

"Often," Rainshadow said. "When we attack sleds carrying human slaves, we free them. That is where the whites among us have come from."

Finn could hardly speak his next question. "Have

51

you . . . have you freed a young girl, in the last few months? A girl named Jena – Jena Ferral. My . . . my sister."

"I do not know her." Rainshadow's voice softened as he saw Finn's face clench with disappointment. "But the Wasteland is large," he went on quickly, "and its people live in small groups, always moving in search of food and shelter, and watching for Slavers. Another group might have freed her, and I would not know about it."

"Then there's a chance," Finn muttered.

"There is," Rainshadow assured him. "And soon you could find out for yourself. The groups often meet together, to hold a council, and talk and plan. Five days from now, there is to be such a council. Come with us, Finn Ferral – " he glanced sideways – "and Baer. Come to the council. If the girl you seek is in the Wasteland, she will be there."

7

Decision

"I'M STAYIN' OUT here," Baer said firmly, "an' that's final."

"You're just being stubborn!" Finn said angrily. They were on their own, at the edge of the oasis, while the Indians were swiftly burying the dead Slavers and erasing the signs of battle.

Baer sighed. "Use your brains, Finn. There's no reason why I should go upsettin' a lotta people. Even these folks here feel a little twitchy round me. An' you'll be worryin' about that when what you want is to have a scout round for your sister . . . "

"They'd get used to you," Finn said.

"Why should they hafta?" Baer said reasonably. "Anyways, bein' with a lotta humans is likely to make me as edgy as I make them. It's better this way, an' it doesn't need to be all that long."

Finn shook his head, aware that he was not winning this argument. "But what will you do?"

"Find me a hidey-hole," Baer said, "somewhere in the desert. Take all the food an' water I need, an' just lie around, eat an' sleep an' get rested up."

"Remember there was a spywing here," Finn reminded him. "This place could be crawling with Slavers soon."

Baer gestured at the busy Indians. "An' they'll find nothin'. You'll be long gone, I'll be hidin' in the Wasteland. So they'll look round awhile an' go home – you know what they're like." He grinned cheerily. "Come on, boy – I was on my own for years 'fore I met you. What's a few days?"

"You didn't have The Claw after you then," Finn muttered.

"He's not after me now," Baer pointed out. "He's after you. An' we've seen no sign of him since the gorge. Anyway, the Wasteland's a big place – wherever The Claw is, I figure I can stay outa his way."

"All right," Finn said, admitting defeat. "I'll tell Rainshadow."

He went to join the Indians, noticing with interest that the open ground beyond the brush showed no sign that anything unusual had happened there. Even the whirlsled had been pushed into the greenery and camouflaged, to hide it from spywings.

When Finn explained Baer's plans, Rainshadow nodded understandingly. "Your friend is wise, and courteous. My people might accept him in time, but would be fearful of him at first. We will leave him all the food and water he needs, and will take him to a place where he will be safe."

So it was decided. And though Finn remained anxious and doubtful, at least the separation was not to be immediate. Rainshadow decided that the group would travel together to the place, several kilometres away, where Baer would remain, and camp there for the night.

By then the Indians had moved away, across the oasis, towards their horses and their two other companions, including the man who had been injured by the heatlance. When Finn, Baer and Rainshadow joined them, Finn saw that the man's arm and shoulder had been badly seared. But the Indians carried healing herbs as well as food and water in bundles slung over their horses' necks, and the man had been well looked after. Finn also noticed that the Indians had brought along the two Slavers' heatlances, which would make a useful addition to their firepower, if it were needed. But more of his attention went on an inspection of the horses.

They were sturdy, powerful little creatures, totally unlike the giant plough-horses that were Finn's only experience of their kind. And just then they were also highly nervous, snorting and trembling, rolling white-rimmed eyes towards Baer.

"There's another reason for me stayin'," Baer grinned. "Tame animals're scared to death of me. Once back east I got too close to a human village with some horses in a field. Those critturs're prob'ly *still* runnin'."

Rainshadow's bright smile flashed. "If you were coming all the way with us, it seems we would have to walk. It will be better if we can move swiftly tomorrow."

"How do we do that?" Finn asked, eyeing the horses dubiously.

"You will ride double with me," Rainshadow said. Then he saw Finn's unease, and smiled again. "So – there is *one* of our skills you have not mastered. Never mind – you will learn."

Despite that unsettling promise, the hours that followed were some of the most enjoyable that Finn had spent since he left his home. As they journeyed – on foot – Rainshadow gave Finn and Baer a swift and fascinating introduction to Wasteland survival: which plants and animals could be safely eaten, where water might be sought, how to read some of the desert's weather signs, and much more. Finn absorbed it all hungrily, now and then offering comparisons with the eastern wilderness. And that led eventually to a change of subject.

The two young humans were intensely curious about one another, but Finn was reluctant to talk about himself. So, Baer took over the conversation, with a colourful version of Finn's life story, as he knew it. And Rainshadow listened with silent amazement as Baer wound up with a blow-by-blow account of their raid on the Slaver base.

When the tale ended, Rainshadow was looking at Finn with something like awe. "Had we not met as we did," he said at last, "I would not believe what I have heard. I am proud to know such a warrior."

Finn flushed as red as the western sky, where the sun was dropping into a fiery sunset. "Don't make me out more than I am," he muttered. "I had a lot of luck – and I had Baer."

"My people say," Rainshadow replied, "that a man fashions his luck from his courage and skill. As for Baer, I would also like to hear his story."

"Any time," Baer rumbled. "But right now, I'm all talked out. I figure it's your turn."

Rainshadow agreed – but was interrupted. They had come to the place where Baer was to stay. It was a narrow, deep trench, on a rocky hillside, almost undetectable by anyone not close to its edge – and offering some jutting shelf-like outcrops that would also protect Baer from prying eyes in the sky. Finn nodded his approval, and also approved of the fact that some of the warriors had been drifting behind them, erasing their trail as skilfully as Finn himself could have done.

But Baer's approval was directed at the other group of Indians who had preceded them. They had made a small smokeless fire, and had produced food from their saddlebags – strips of dried meat, and chunks of flat bread that Finn found solid but tasty. So they rested, and ate, as the night enveloped them, while Rainshadow told them about the warriors of the Wasteland.

He reached back into history to tell of his people as they had been in the Forgotten Time – divided into tribal groups, living wretched lives on barren patches of land where they had been thrust by the push of white civilization. "Once the Indian lived as a part of nature," he said, "belonging to the land as the coyote or the eagle belong. But the white man lived apart from nature, and was a foolish, destructive enemy to the land."

"An' to himself," Baer rumbled.

Rainshadow nodded, and spoke of the end of the Forgotten Time, with its rain of fire, as the tales of his people remembered

56

it. Some of the western Indians found survival in the mountains – but were driven from that refuge, centuries later, by the coming of the Slavers. So they fled to the desert, found that the aliens would not pursue them there, and used their ancient wilderness skills to create a life of peace and freedom for all its harshness.

Much had changed for them, of course. The old divisions of tribe and clan had faded – so that Rainshadow himself bore the blood of several long-forgotten peoples, Navajo, Hopi, Apache. Today the desert Indians were one united people, numbering not more than about a thousand. And over the many lifetimes since the Slavers had come, about a thousand more, non-Indians, had joined them – freed slaves, a few daring wanderers seeking a refuge – and had adapted swiftly to desert life.

Now the people of the Wasteland lived in small groups, wandering as nomads in the ancient way, but united in a loose confederation that met together when important decisions were to be made. It had a central council, advisors rather than rulers, of which Rainshadow had lately become a member. And he added that one of its senior members, a man named Corwin, had spent his life gathering, wherever he could, as much knowledge as he could find of the ancient days, the Forgotten Time – and knowledge also of the Earth's alien masters. It was largely because of Corwin that the people of the Wasteland dreamed a long-term dream – to rebuild human civilization, in a world freed from Slavers.

Baer laughed sourly at the idea. "If that ever happened, people'd just start killin' each other off again."

Rainshadow shrugged. "Now it is still a dream, but it means much to Corwin. He speaks constantly of a day when we will march out of the Wasteland, and rouse humanity to fight a final war against the Slavers. And such dreams are needed, to keep the human spirit alive."

"Maybe so," Finn said doubtfully. "But it's not likely to come true. I'll stick to my own dream, of finding Jena and getting my family together again."

Rainshadow smiled faintly. "What you have done in pursuit of your dream is not so different from what we do, fighting the Slavers in pursuit of ours."

Finn frowned, but before he could reply Baer yawned hugely. "You young fellas can argue about that if you like. Me, I'm gonna pursue a few dreams of my own – the sleepin' kind."

Rainshadow laughed. "We should all sleep. We have much travelling to do, tomorrow."

So they made themselves comfortable by the dwindling fire. But sleep did not come at once to Finn. He lay for a long while staring up at the star-filled desert sky, mulling over the strangenesses that had come into his life.

He had always felt alone, except for Josh and Jena, in the village where he had grown up – because he was too *different* to find friends among the narrow and fearful villagers. Oddly, it had not been until he was totally alone, in his search for his family, that he had found his first real friend, in Baer. But even then the two of them had remained alone, because of what they were, and what they were doing. Now, though, he could see that things could change, if he wished it.

He knew that he and Rainshadow would be friends. He also knew that he felt more at home with the wild desert Indians than with any other humans he had known. But somehow he wanted to *resist* that feeling. He was here to look for Jena, not to find a home for himself. It was even possible that there was no place he could ever call home.

But the thought did not trouble him, just then. He did not want to think beyond the present, and the new hope he had been offered. As he drifted into sleep, all that mattered to him was the chance that, somewhere in this desert, his long and tortuous search for Jena might come to an end.

He was up at daybreak with the others, and he and Baer sat idly, chewing lumps of the solid bread, watching the Indians swiftly readying their horses for travel. Finn felt increasingly heavy-hearted, reluctant to leave Baer but knowing that he would have to do so. And it seemed all too soon when Rainshadow came over to tell him it was time to go.

"Just keep your head down," Finn told Baer firmly. "And we'll cover our trail when we leave."

"Thanks," Baer grinned. "I'd as soon not have The Claw disturbin' my rest."

He had spoken casually, but the effect on Rainshadow was startling. His face seemed to go grey beneath its copper-brown hue. "The Claw?" he said sharply. "What do you know of The Claw?"

Finn and Baer looked at each other uneasily. "Guess we never got that far in the story-tellin'," Baer rumbled. "The Claw, he's . . . sorta chasin' us." Swiftly he recounted what had happened before they entered the Wasteland.

"Do you know about The Claw?" Finn asked Rainshadow, who was growing more and more disturbed.

"We know him," the Indian said bleakly. "The most cruel and dangerous servant of the Slavers." His dark eyes stared past them, as if seeing a distant vision of horror. "Once The Claw led a force of Bloodkin into the Wasteland, to put an end to our attacks on Slavers. At first the people stood and fought, and many died. Then we scattered, hoping to weaken The Claw's force by striking from ambush. But The Claw is skilled and deadly, as if he too is a creature of the wilderness, and it was he who ambushed us. It was like making war against the desert wind."

A strange, chanting tone had entered Rainshadow's voice, and Finn's scalp crawled. "What happened?"

"The Wasteland defeated him," Rainshadow said simply. "We fled to hide in the worst, most terrible regions. And The Claw would have pursued us even there – but his Bloodkin were not as skilled as he. They suffered from heat and thirst and

59

exhaustion – and in the end The Claw had to pull back before too many of his army deserted or died."

"Too bad the Wasteland didn't get to him," Baer growled.

Rainshadow shook his head. "The Claw is as much at home in the wilds as I, or any of us. Or as you, Finn. And now you say he is on your trail, which will lead him again to the Wasteland."

"We didn't lead him here on purpose," Baer growled.

Rainshadow made a pacifying gesture. "I am not saying you are at fault. But if The Claw is near, perhaps with another army, the people must know at once." A deep sadness invaded his voice. "It will be as before. We must risk death in the heart of the Wasteland, or face a more certain death at the hands of The Claw."

8

Separation

RAINSHADOW WENT AT once to confer with his men, holding the horses some distance away from Baer. In moments the Indians were leaping on to their mounts, galloping away in swirls of dust – all but two of them, who remained, watching impassively as Rainshadow joined Finn.

"My warriors will ride into the Wasteland," he explained, "to seek other groups and bring them this evil news. The word will spread from group to group while they gather for the council. These two – " he gestured to the pair that had remained – "will cover our tracks a while, then will ride out as well."

Finn nodded, then turned awkwardly to take his leave of Baer. But the big Bloodkin simply clapped him bruisingly on the shoulder and shooed him away. "No sense wastin' the mornin' sayin' g'bye," he rumbled. They grinned at each other for a moment, and then, with a cheery wave to Rainshadow, Baer lumbered stolidly away along the cleft.

Finn watched him for a moment, with a lump in his throat and a distinct feeling of unreality. Then he turned away and, urged on by Rainshadow, clambered nervously on to the back of the horse behind the young Indian.

"Now," Rainshadow said, "we *ride*."

The sturdy little horse seemed not at all troubled by the extra weight, and maintained a smooth gallop as the kilometres began to roll by. But Finn always seemed to be slipping sideways, or to be clumsily bounced and jolted on the horse's muscled back. And it did not help that Rainshadow seemed part of the horse, riding with a fluid grace that filled Finn with envy.

The first day wore away into tedium and weariness, interrupted only by too-brief pauses to rest the horse or to snatch a mouthful of food, a gulp of water. At the day's end, Finn crawled from the horse feeling a hundred years old, sore and aching in every joint and muscle. He had no trouble sleeping that night – but he did not find it so easy, stiff and cramped in the morning, to face another day's tormented travel.

Yet during that day his body began to work out what it should be doing. Instinctively he had begun to adjust to the horse's motion – and as he grew more confident, he was able to take some notice of his surroundings. The land had been growing even more rugged – steeper hills, huger outcrops of naked rock, scatterings of enormous boulders that were sometimes heaped upon one another in looming, treacherously balanced piles. But there were also occasional patches of the Wasteland's strange vegetation, in the hollows, which allowed Rainshadow to expand on his lessons in desert survival – and Finn drank them up as avidly as he did the occasional, sparing sips of water.

By the end of that second day's almost non-stop riding, his muscles no longer seemed to ache quite so sorely. And he was noticeably more cheerful when they crested a steep ridge and found themselves, to Finn's surprise, entering a gully that held several small, oddly-shaped dwellings, and a scattering of people.

"The rest of my own group," Rainshadow explained, "waiting for me before we set off for the council."

Finn dismounted, gazing curiously around. It was a long time since he had been in a human village – and to his eyes this was a very odd village. The dwellings were low tents, cone-shaped, made of hides wrapped round a frame of light poles. Among them cooking fires blossomed, with a few plain implements beside them, and behind the tents a small herd of horses was quietly tethered. But Finn was looking with more interest at the people – about twenty of them, mostly young women and children and some older adults – who had crowded near, staring at Finn with equal curiosity and interest.

Rainshadow paused for a moment to speak to a young warrior, and Finn recognized the man as the one who had been hurt at the oasis – and whose arm was freshly bandaged. Then Rainshadow turned to the others.

"This is the man," he said, indicating Finn, "who stopped my raiding party from walking into a Slaver trap. He is a warrior of courage and skill. I call him friend, and brother, and wish him to be made welcome."

The people seemed happy to do as he asked. They gathered round Finn, and took him to their hearts. He was led to a fireside, plied with sweet water for his thirst and a bewildering array of food for his hunger. Rainshadow joined him, and something of a celebration began as the evening descended. If the group knew about the threat of The Claw, they seemed to have chosen not to mention it. Instead, it was a night of merry talk, laughter, some strange Indian songs. And, despite the strangeness, once again Finn began to realize that he had never felt so much at home as among these wild but warmly friendly desert folk.

After some hours the others slipped away to their tents, and Finn sat with Rainshadow, feeling fatigue settling on him like a blanket.

"I'm grateful," Finn said awkwardly. "They all made me feel welcome."

"So you will be among any of the Wasteland people," Rainshadow said, "when the word has spread."

"I hope your men will spread word about Baer, too," Finn replied. "I wouldn't want another group of your people to find him and attack him."

"It will not happen," Rainshadow assured him. "One of the

two men who came after us will remain in the desert, near Baer, to watch over him. Baer will not see him – and I did not mention it, for fear Baer would be insulted."

"He might, at that," Finn smiled. "I'm grateful again."

Rainshadow shook his head. "It is a small thing. I am still in your debt, for what you did at the oasis."

"Help me find Jena," Finn said, "and I'll be in *your* debt."

Rainshadow pointed towards the south-west. "Two days' ride from here is the place of the council. By the time we reach it, most of the Wasteland people will·be there. Then we shall see."

In a few moments Finn and Rainshadow made their way towards the tents. And at the same time, many kilometres away, Baer too was readying himself for a night's sleep. He had made no fire, but he had feasted on the Indians' dried meat and bread, and was now – as he had done the night before – moving with wary caution along the sloping wall of the cleft, peering out at the Wasteland.

He was not expecting to see any danger, but was merely having a routine look around. His caution arose from the moonless darkness of the night, more deeply black within the cleft, which made him unsure of his footing. When he stubbed his toe for the second time, he cursed in a muffled rumble and scrambled up out of the cleft, to amble peacefully along on the more level ground by its edge.

He did not know that, some while before, a copper-skinned rider had made a wide and similarly wary circle around the cleft, swinging far out into the desert. Nor did Baer know that the rider was now crouching behind a dune, only a short distance away, grinning to himself as he listened to Baer's low cursing and noisy scramble.

But neither Baer nor his unseen Indian guard were aware of another pair of eyes nearby – eyes that were able to see equally well by night or day, and that had at once spotted Baer's shadowy bulk as it emerged over the lip of the cleft. Eyes that bulged glassily from the head of a small creature drifting through the darkness on wings that were silent as an owl's, but shaped like a bat's.

At first light Finn was roused by noisy activity outside his tent, and emerged to watch with interest as the Indians, swiftly and efficiently, stowed away their camp. In moments the tents became bundles on the backs of pack horses, with the poles and other articles neatly fastened around them. Nomads, Finn realized, own little and travel light. As did people who were pursued, he reminded himself.

After a hasty breakfast, he found himself on the back of a horse of his own, whose hide showed alternating patches of brown and white, and who seemed to look round at him with some amusement.

"Riding by yourself is less difficult," Rainshadow called, grinning. "The horse knows what to do."

And so it proved. As the group moved off at a steady canter, Finn's horse fell in with them, though he had failed to direct it. And as the hours and kilometres spun away, Finn found that it *was* easier to find the rhythm of the horse's stride, and adjust to it. By mid-afternoon he was even winning a few approving nods, as well as smiles, from the others. And so they went along steadily, with only few and brief rests, deeper into the Wasteland.

By nightfall they halted in the shelter of one of the huge, tumbled heaps of boulders. They did not make camp, and made a sparing supper of dried meat, but Finn was not troubled. One more day, he was saying to himself – and the excitement and hope that gripped him overshadowed all thought of weariness or discomfort.

But back at the cleft in the depths of the desert, no one was feeling excited. Baer had spent the day half-asleep in the shade of an out-cropping – and the warrior guarding him had grown restless. In the late afternoon, riding out on another watchful sweep of the land around the cleft, he decided to venture farther to the north-west, just to break the routine.

Late afternoon found him flattened on a ridge, wide-eyed and sweating, wishing desperately that routine had remained uninterrupted.

In the distance, moving in the midst of a dust cloud, was the army of The Claw. The Indian saw the vague shapes of a horde of savage Bloodkin, and behind them what seemed to be another horde of oddly-dressed humans. But even more terrible, at the head of the advancing column, he saw the menacing, ovoid shapes of four alien whirlsleds.

He did not wait for the column to draw closer. He sprang for his horse and kicked it into a furious gallop. Baer had to be warned.

He could not have known that he would be too late.

Around the cleft, the shadows of twilight were deepening among the scattered rocks and ridges. And other shadows were moving among them. A half-dozen dark-furred Bloodkin, stepping with silent, painstaking care in the wake of their tall, smooth-skinned, cat-footed leader. At the edge of the cleft they halted, crouching among the rocks in obedience to their leader's gestures.

Within the cleft, Baer was feeling bored. Dozing in the shade was all very well, he thought, but he had grown too used to activity in the months with Finn. It was time to have a wander around, while it was not yet full dark, and see what he could see. He set off along the cleft, towards the place where he had scrambled out, the previous night.

Moments later, he was on the edge of the cleft, gazing serenely around at the bleak and empty desert. The shadows among the rocks around him were just shadows.

66

Until they erupted into six snarling Bloodkin who hurled themselves ferociously upon him.

Bellowing with shock and rage, Baer was quick enough to draw his machete, and to feel its edge bite deep into shaggy flesh. But then the weight of numbers bore him down – and though he struggled heroically, at last he was pinned, motionless, staring up at a glittering knife-blade flashing down towards his throat.

Less than a hundred metres away, invisible in the darkness, the Indian guard was staring as well, trembling with horror, guilt and rage. He had crept stealthily forward in time to see the savage attack – and he was clutching his spear, on the verge of charging the bestial attackers in a suicidal attempt to stop that descending blade.

But he was frozen where he crouched by a cold voice that cracked like a whip, and also held the knife-blade in mid-air as if it had struck an unseen wall.

"Alive, curse you!" shouted The Claw. "I want him alive!"

That was enough for the watching Indian. Almost weeping with anger and bitter self-reproach, he turned and fled noiselessly towards his horse. And beside the cleft, The Claw lifted his head a moment, listening. Then he looked down again, smiling thinly into Baer's furious scowl.

"If you continue to struggle," the cold voice said, "my men will cripple you. Permanently."

"Why not just kill me an' get it done?" Baer growled.

The Claw's eyes glittered. "You are bait, renegade. For your young friend."

"He won't even know you got me," Baer snorted, "an' he's not fool enough to walk into a trap of yours."

The Claw paused before replying. In the silence, even Baer could hear the faint drumming of a horse's hooves, fading into the distance.

The Claw's smile widened slightly. "The watcher has gone to bear the sad news," he said. "And I am sure your friend will come. Remember, renegade, he walked into a trap before, because of you."

He turned away, gesturing to the Bloodkin. "Bind his arms and bring him. If he gives trouble, spill some of his blood. So long as it is not fatal."

9

Reunion

DURING THE SECOND day of their journey to the place of the council, Rainshadow's people slowed the pace a little, resting the horses more often. Finn was grateful, for the journey was taking a particular toll on his energies, already drained by his and Baer's almost non-stop flight from the mountains. Yet he was also growing impatient for the journey to end. As the rocky desolation of the Wasteland rolled on interminably around them, he was beginning to feel that he had been condemned to ride forever across the same arid landscape, under the unchanging glare of the sky.

But finally, in the late afternoon, Rainshadow pointed to a distant hilltop, glinting golden in the slanting rays of the sun. "The gathering place," he said. "Just beyond there."

Those remaining kilometres seemed the longest of all. Then at last they breasted the hilltop, and excitement swept over Finn like a shower of cool water, sweeping weariness away. The place of the council was a wide-floored gully with enough vegetation to show that it held a water supply. And in the gully hundreds of people were gathered, sitting, strolling, chatting, eating.

As they rode down the sloping side of the gully, Finn spared only a glance for the scattered scores of tents, most now with their own cooking fires, and the hundreds of horses standing within a corral of ropes strung between stakes driven into the ground. He could not take his eyes from the people. And though he felt uneasy, for he had never before confronted such a large crowd, he also felt an almost dizzying surge of hope. His gaze probed the crowd, searching for the reality of the image that had never left his mind for all the past months – the image of a small, slim girl with long fair hair and laughing eyes as blue as the summer sky.

As they entered the camp, an uproar of shouts and greetings swelled around them. People ran to gather around Rainshadow, calling to him with a cheery affection. In the regard that the people clearly felt for the young Indian, Finn had a new insight into this strange community. Though they might live in separate, wandering groups, they were closely bound – by their way of life and their common enemy. And the regular council gatherings served, in part, to reaffirm that closeness. Finn felt an intruder within this warm and merry reunion.

But then he found that the warmth extended to him, as well – which meant that Rainshadow's men had successfully spread the word. He too was greeted enthusiastically, by name, though also with a respectful curiosity. But the people could see that he was weary and dazed and preoccupied, and soon they courteously withdrew, leaving him in peace, to gather himself. Rainshadow vanished into the midst of a large group whose grim faces showed that they were mainly concerned with the news about The Claw. So Finn simply wandered among the people, looking, listening, asking one question that was important to him.

But he soon became glumly aware that what he was searching for was not there. The few small, blonde, blue-eyed girls he had seen were strangers. And no one had heard the name Jena.

By the time a sliver of moon had ventured into the night sky, Rainshadow found Finn sitting alone near the horses, staring into emptiness, silent and miserable.

The young Indian's face twisted with sympathy. "Some groups have not yet come in," he told Finn gently. "There is still a chance."

70

Finn nodded bleakly. "That's all there ever was . . . " he broke off, staring intently at the far hillside. Another group of riders had appeared, and the crowd was again rushing to greet them. But the firelight showed no young blonde girls among the newcomers, and Finn sagged back into dejection.

"Corwin's group – at last!" Rainshadow said happily. "I will bring him to meet you."

At that Finn sat up a little. Rainshadow had spoken of this man, who possessed so much knowledge of the ancient past. Despite his gloom, Finn very much wanted to meet Corwin.

And Corwin proved just as eager to meet Finn. When Rainshadow returned, he brought with him a small, round-faced, smiling man, egg-bald save for a fringe of grey hair, whose skin was a surprising dark brown – like many others, Finn recalled, in the crowd that occupied the gully. Finn found himself responding with a grin as Corwin shook his hand vigorously.

"Wonderful to meet you!" he said cheerily. "Ever since I heard about you and your Bloodkin friend, my head has been buzzing! There is so much you can tell us . . . "

Rainshadow laughed. "Corwin, your head is always buzzing. But there will be time for talk. We have not yet eaten, and are weary from travel."

Corwin beamed merrily. "It is always this way – people putting trivialities in the way of we who seek knowledge. Come, Rainshadow, you may invite me to supper, and we will talk as we eat. If Finn does not mind . . . ?"

"I'd be glad of it," Finn said quickly. "My head's full of questions, too. Especially one."

Humour gave way to sympathy on Corwin's round face. "I know. You seek a young girl – your sister. And I regret that I do not know if she is in the Wasteland. But there are several groups still to come in, I hear."

"So I have told him," Rainshadow put in. "We must wait, and hope. And while we do so, we must eat – and talk, before

71

the buzzing in Corwin's head drives him completely mad!"

An hour later, a large meal had been reduced to crumbs, and Finn and Corwin were deep in conversation. Corwin was fascinated by the story of Finn's quest across the land, but most of all by his daring raid on the Slaver base where Josh had been held. Time and again he asked a penetrating question about the details – the layout of the base, the machines and equipment. But Finn could give only vague answers, for the alien technology had been a mystery to him.

"Baer should be here," he said at last. "He knows more about Slavers than I ever will."

"I hope to meet him," Corwin replied eagerly. "His knowledge would be priceless."

Finn smiled. "From what Rainshadow told me, I thought you already knew just about everything."

"Not by a long way," Corwin chuckled. "But for me, acquiring knowledge – learning things – is the very purpose of being alive. There is always something to learn."

Finn thought briefly of old Josh, who had felt much the same way, and who had taught Finn the basics of reading and writing, and what little else he could manage, besides a huntsman's skills. "I think I'd like to learn things, know things," he said wistfully.

"What, for instance?" Corwin smiled.

Finn shrugged. "I don't know. About the Forgotten Time – or what the Slavers are, why they came – *where* they came from . . . "

"That, at least, I can tell you," Corwin said. "They came from another planet – another world."

He pointed up to the night sky, and gave Finn a swift, crisp astronomy lesson, about stars and planets, suns and worlds. Finn was not sure he understood it all, but he was delighted. And Corwin was just as pleased at finding such an eager,

72

attentive pupil. He talked on, moving easily from astronomy to history. And he proved to be one of those wonderful teachers who can explain the most complex matters in simple and clear terms, bringing them alive in the listener's mind. Finn was enthralled.

Corwin described what he knew of life in the Forgotten Time, how the rulers of mighty nations vied with one another for domination, and eventually went to war. He spoke of monstrous weapons called bombs, and the lethal poison they spread called radiation. Vast numbers of weapons had been placed in the western deserts of this land, he said, and the enemy had struck at them with such fury that the very terrain had been changed forever, as well as the living creatures of what was now the Wasteland.

He spoke of the survivors of that war, skulking amid ash and rubble and the leftover deadliness of radioactivity. And in passing he even answered Finn's questions about the People of the Gorge. They descended, he said, from a fanatically religious group who had abandoned the world and its evils, to live wretched and self-punishing lives in the caves they had dug in the gorge's cliffs. When they survived the holocaust, they believed they had been specially "chosen" – and their descendants still believed it when the Slavers came to Earth. But the Slavers had ignored them until, in more recent times, The Claw had found them and turned their fanaticism to his own dire uses.

Corwin spoke also of the coming of the Slavers, and confirmed what Finn had been told by Baer – that the aliens had come to plunder what was left of the wondrous metals created by humanity in the Forgotten Time. "That is why they ignore the Wasteland," he said. "Because almost nothing is left, after the holocaust. And what metals can still be found are usually still radioactive, which the Slavers seem to fear."

That statement stirred an old curiosity in Finn's mind. "I've wondered," he said hesitantly, "if the Slavers are really alive, like we are – or if they're like the spywings, inside."

Corwin nodded approvingly. "That question fascinates me as well. But I cannot answer it. The casing of a Slaver body will resist even a heatlance, so I have never dissected one. It is most frustrating."

Finn agreed, without being quite sure what "dissect" meant. For a moment Corwin was silent, lost in thought, and in that moment Finn was suddenly overtaken by a huge yawn. At once Corwin was shamefaced and apologetic.

"I've kept you up far too long," he said guiltily. "Rainshadow told me how fatigued you are – I have been thoughtless."

Finn brushed the apology away. "I wouldn't have missed it," he said honestly. "I don't understand how you know so much."

"My forebears," Corwin explained. "After the Forgotten Time an ancestor – a very knowledgeable man – preserved many books, and much information. It has been handed down, father to son, ever since. And more knowledge has been gleaned, over the years, from what other people could learn, or could remember – as I have gleaned from you."

"I wish I could see those books," Finn said idly, with another vast yawn.

"You can, easily," Corwin replied at once. "But that is something we can speak of in the morning."

So they said their good nights, and Finn went wearily in search of Rainshadow, to find directions to the tent he would use. And when at last he was stretched out upon a bed of soft hides and furs, he thought for a moment about everything that Corwin had told him – and how good it would be to look at Corwin's books, and to learn more answers to the questions that always plagued his curiosity. But that would mean staying in the Wasteland, he thought. And instantly the image of Jena formed in his mind, as if to chide him for even thinking of abandoning his quest. But then all thoughts and images faded, and sleep struck him like a club.

He awoke at sunrise, but did not get up at once, feeling in no hurry to go out among the throng of people. The images of the night before returned, and he felt only a vague regret at the thought that he would probably be leaving the gathering during that day. If Jena was not among any of the late-coming groups – and there was not much chance, he told himself glumly, that she was – he would go and find Baer, and they would resume their journey to the western mountains. But then if Jena *was* with one of the groups . . .

He sat up with a slight feeling of shock. If she was, *what?* He realized for the first time that he had never really thought about what to do when he had got his family together again. If he ever did. . . .

As always, he pushed that thought firmly away. And then he understood that *that* was why he had never thought much about the future. Because deep within himself he knew just how unlikely it was that he would find Jena alive. So he had never let himself think about how his quest might end. He had just gone doggedly on, day by day, moment by moment, hardly thinking at all.

I wish I could talk to Baer right now, he thought gloomily. But then he shook himself, angrily trying to drive away the black mood that threatened to grip him, and rose to his feet. As he did so, Rainshadow appeared in the tent's opening, grinning widely. And Finn began to realize that a considerable tumult had sprung up outside – much like the noise that had greeted his and Rainshadow's arrival.

"What's all the shouting?" Finn asked.

"Marakela has just ridden in," the young Indian said. "Come – you must meet her."

"Her?" Finn asked wonderingly, following Rainshadow out of the tent.

Then he stopped. A large crowd was moving in his direction, full of laughter and loud talk. In the forefront he saw Corwin, and next to him a tall, broad-shouldered woman with a shock of bright red hair who was laughing like a deep, resonant bell.

"That is Marakela," Rainshadow said. He seemed oddly excited. "A great warrior, as are all her women."

"Women?" Finn repeated, as blankly as before.

"Marakela suffered much at the hands of the Slavers, before she was freed," Rainshadow explained. "Now her band of warriors is made up of women, whom she has freed from the same suffering."

Finn's heart seemed to stop, and no words would come. But by then there was no need to speak, for the crowd had come close enough for him to hear what the big red-headed woman was saying to Corwin.

" . . . ridin' in from the east, slow an' easy," she was booming. "Then we met a fella who tole us the news, an' we dam' near killed the horses gettin' here."

Finn only half-listened, for his eyes were avidly searching the crowd. Among it he could see several other women dressed much like Marakela – thigh-length tunics, light boots, with knives at their belts and sturdy bows and arrows slung at their backs. All of them looked dust-covered and exhausted, but still they were smiling as they looked at Finn.

"Why'd y' ride so hard?" Finn heard a cheerful voice yell from the crowd. "Hungry fer male company?"

Marakela's deep laugh rang out again. "Not fer yours, bigmouth!" Her eyes swung back to fix on Finn. "Nope, we came runnin' when we heard 'bout the stranger." Her grin broadened as if at some private joke. "Might say a devil was drivin' us. This devil."

She reached back, grasped one of her band by the shoulder, and thrust her forward. The one who had been so roughly produced stumbled, then caught herself and straightened. Finn saw a small, deeply tanned, muscular but shapely young woman, dressed and armed like the others. Dust masked her face and streaked her short, sun-bleached hair. But then she took another step forward, and Finn found himself staring into eyes that were brimming with tears, and that were as blue as the summer sky.

"Finn?" Jena said. "Don't you know me?"

PART THREE

Canyon of Blood

10

Council

THE MORNING SPED past, hours seeming like minutes. Once the boisterous shared delight of the crowd had spent itself, Finn and Jena had drifted away, finding a patch of shade beneath some gnarled trees. There they talked as if they had been starved for speech, and still always there seemed too much to say.

Jena was overflowing with questions about Finn's adventures, which he answered as best he could – bringing her to tears again, with relief, when he told her that Josh was safe and on his way westwards. And Finn was just as full of questions about the ordeal of Jena's captivity, and her escape.

But she remembered only fragments of the days after she and Josh were taken. Most of the time, she had been in a mindless state of shock, which had grown worse when she and Josh were separated. But before then, she remembered Josh muttering his firm belief that Finn would come after them.

"He hoped you wouldn't," Jena said, shivering, "because he said you'd be killed. He said death would be the best thing for him and me, but you needed a chance to live."

Still, Jena had not died, even through the numbing, endless days of travel, huddled in the back of a whirlsled behind her silent, alien captors. Heat and thirst had vied with shock and terror to weaken her – so that she had been barely aware when, at last, the sled was attacked.

A band of riders, on the edge of the Wasteland, had ridden into the open, tempting the Slavers to pursue, and had led the whirlsled in a chase that had ended at the edge of a narrow, hidden trench. The horses leaped the gap, but the whirlsled, hovering on its energy cushion, toppled over the edge and split open like the egg it resembled. Jena had been struck unconscious in the crash, and had awakened on the back of a horse, being supported by a laughing, red-haired giant of a woman.

In the months since then she had been part of Marakela's band, learning to ride, to use a bow, to survive in the desert, to live as a free and fearless warrior of the Wasteland.

"So it's no wonder you didn't recognize me at first," she said with a laugh.

"But you're still Jena," Finn said firmly. "And when we find Josh, the three of us will be together again, like we used to be."

Jena looked at him for a silent moment. "Can we do that?" she asked at last. "I think too much has happened, to all of us. We couldn't go back to some hideaway village in the forest, and be the same as we were. Not knowing what we do, now, about the way the world is."

Finn stared at her, shaken. "I suppose . . . I haven't thought about it much. All I've dreamed about is getting the three of us together again, and safe."

"I know." Jena rested a small hand on his arm. "And you made your dream come true, which is . . . nearly a miracle. But we can't simply go away, on our own. There's nowhere we could be safe – you know that. Nowhere but here."

Finn blinked. "You mean we should stay in the Wasteland?"

"Where else?" Jena said. "I can't leave Marakela and the others. I owe them my life – and I'm one of them. And you could be, too, Finn. This is where we *both* belong."

"I entirely agree," said a voice behind them.

Finn turned and saw the small brown figure of Corwin, with Rainshadow beside him.

81

"Forgive us for intruding," Corwin said, "but the council will soon begin, and there are things still to be said between us, Finn."

Finn looked at him numbly. He was staggered by what Jena had said, and for a moment had been left speechless.

"Tell him," Jena said to Corwin. "Tell him why he should stay with us."

"That can be told quite simply," Corwin replied. "We need him." He turned to Finn, his expression earnest. "From what I hear of you, young man, you are a special person. You have unique abilities in the wilds, you have survived dangers that most of us would tremble to think about, and you have more direct knowledge of the Slavers than anyone here. That knowledge could benefit us greatly, if we are to oppose them."

Finn stared, as if he could not believe what he was hearing. "Rainshadow spoke about a war against the Slavers, but I thought it was just a dream. You talk as if you're really *planning* it."

"So we are," Corwin said. "Someday humans will have to rise up against the Slavers, or lose their humanity forever. And *we* will have to spearhead that rising – the warriors of the Wasteland, who have always fought the aliens."

"And how soon," Finn asked bluntly, "is this *someday*?"

Corwin smiled wryly. "Not soon. We need more people, and better weapons. We have only spears and arrows, and a few heatlances taken from attacks on whirlsleds. But we also need to know more about the enemy. That is why you and your friend Baer would be welcome – for your prowess as warriors, and your knowledge."

Finn looked slowly from one to another of the three faces, watching him intently. "I don't know what you're talking about. I didn't come to fight any wars. I came to find Jena, and get her and Josh somewhere where we can be together. That's all."

"But, Finn," Jena said softly, pleadingly, "I don't want to go.

82

And I don't think Josh will, either, when he gets here."

For another long moment Finn stared at them, bewildered, troubled, but with a small flare of anger visible in his eyes. "Listen," he burst out. "I'm not good with words, but what you're saying makes no sense. I'm just one person – I can't win or lose a war for you. But I do know the difference between attacking Slavers now and then, one or two at a time, and marching out to take *all* of them on, in a real war. You wouldn't stand a chance. They'd wipe you out in a day." He swept his angry gaze across them. "I'm starting to wonder if you're not all a little crazy. You're talking about fighting a war against all the Slavers – and at the same time you're scared to death because The Claw is around somewhere!"

Corwin chuckled quietly. "Expressed like that, it does sound insane. Of course we are nowhere near to being ready to fight the Slavers – and The Claw is a much more immediate threat."

Rainshadow, who had been silent throughout the conversation, nodded vigorously. "That is really what we came to talk about. We need to know where The Claw is, and the size of his force. After the council, I am taking my best men out in a scouting party. I hoped you would come with us, Finn."

Finn's anger had subsided, and he shrugged and nodded. "All right. But at the same time I'll go and find Baer. I need to talk to him – about all this."

"What do the rest of us do, meanwhile?" Jena asked.

"I believe we should begin a withdrawal," Corwin said sombrely. "Many people agree with me that it would be wise to seek refuge in the Firesands."

Finn looked puzzled. "Firesands?"

"The malignant heart of the Wasteland," Corwin said. As swiftly and crisply as in his talk the night before, he described to Finn a place in the central desert that suffered the worst effects of that final war that ended the Forgotten Time – a place where some of those effects continued still. He described monstrous mutants, regions that looked like lakes of dark glass, other areas where the very sands glowed with deadly radiation, like fire.

Finn shivered. "I think I'd rather face The Claw."

"So would many others, like Marakela," Rainshadow said. "It will depend on the size of his force. But if we must withdraw, we know some safe paths in the Firesands, where he may not dare to pursue us. He will have learned, from the last time, to prepare his forces for desert fighting – but they will not be prepared for the Firesands."

Finn stared thoughtfully into the distance. "Maybe running or fighting aren't the only choices . . . "

"What do you mean?" Jena asked quickly.

He looked at her with a strange emptiness in his eyes that made her feel chilled. "The Claw is here," he said, "because the Slavers want *me*. So maybe . . . "

"Don't even think it!" Jena said, horrified.

"Quite so," Corwin agreed. "The Claw is here because he is The Claw. He may seek you as well, Finn, but we have all known that he would come against us again, someday."

"I don't know . . . " Finn began. But then there was no more time for their private talk. The camp filled with a growing rumble, as all the people began to crowd together in readiness for the start of the council.

The crowd gathered in a wide circle, with a space at its centre where the councillors could be seen by all. Finn and Jena joined the fringes of the throng, while Rainshadow and Corwin went to join the small group of councillors, who included Marakela and a few other older folk. It was an orderly meeting, yet relaxed and communal. Each councillor had his or her say, but also willingly listened when someone from the crowd spoke up to put a point of view.

From the outset it was clear that the majority favoured a strategic retreat from The Claw – though fiery Marakela spoke for a determined group that wanted to stand and fight. And an even smaller minority had another idea, put forward by a fat, bearded man.

"I hear tell," the man said, "that The Claw's here 'cause of the stranger – whatshisname, Finn. Seems t' me purty stupid fer us t' go gettin' killed on account of one stranger."

Jena felt Finn tense beside her, at this echo of his own self-blame. She was about to reply angrily, but Rainshadow forestalled her.

"It is no fault of Finn's," he said sternly. "The Claw came before, yet Finn was not here. Now The Claw has come again. Who is at fault if lightning strikes, or disease comes to a camp?"

A general roar of agreement rose from the crowd, within which Marakela could be heard offering to clarify the fat man's thinking with a punch in the mouth. As the fat man subsided, Corwin quickly outlined the proposal that Rainshadow should lead a scouting party while the others began a withdrawal towards the Firesands.

"We may not even need to enter," he added. "We do not yet know the size of The Claw's force, or which direction he is moving. Perhaps . . ."

But then he broke off. A cloud of dust had appeared on the hilltop overlooking the council, and out of it a horseman came thundering down the slope. He was swaying, nearly falling – and his horse, sweat-lathered, was staggering as if its legs had turned to rubber. As the crowd stared, the horse stumbled and fell, flinging his rider off, and both lay where they fell, chests heaving, as the people rushed towards them.

Finn and Jena were among those nearest, and it was Jena who snatched a water bottle from a nearby belt and poured a few drops on to the man's cracked and dusty lips. But Finn stood motionless, frozen. He had recognized the man as one of Rainshadow's warriors – and knew, with rising horror, that he must be the one who was left to watch over Baer.

But then horror was gripping all the crowd, as the man told them what he had seen, when he spied on The Claw's force.

85

"Many Bloodkin," he gasped. "A hundred or more . . . with heatlances. And others . . . humans . . . "

"*Humans?*" The crowd shouted the word in one voice, shocked and outraged.

"More than half a hundred," the man said. "Strange clothes . . . like dresses . . . "

"The People of the Gorge," Finn said quietly, his words lost in the hubbub around him.

"And worse," the man was continuing. "Slavers . . . four whirlsleds . . . "

That silenced the crowd completely.

"That settles it," Corwin said. "We might have faced the rest of them, even with their weapons, for we would outnumber them considerably. But we cannot face Slavers in whirlsleds – not with The Claw to guide their tactics . . . "

Rainshadow broke in urgently. "How long do we have? Where did you see them?"

"More than . . . three days away," the man croaked. "But The Claw . . . nearer, with Bloodkin. I saw them . . . capture the Bloodkin who is the friend of Finn."

Jena gasped, and everyone nearby turned to look at Finn. He was stricken and pale, and a bitter fury glared from his eyes.

"I should never have left him." Finn's voice was harsh, unrecognizable. "I put him into danger – just as I've put all of you into danger."

"Finn, no – " Jena began. But then the man on the ground moaned, and she turned back to give him more water, while Rainshadow busied himself arranging for others to look after the exhausted man and his half-dead horse. By the time they looked around again, Finn was no longer there.

At once they flung themselves into the crowd, searching. The people had begun to drift away, huddled into small, worried groups. None of them had seen Finn – and as she continued to search, Jena knew with a panicky certainty that she would not find him.

Shortly Rainshadow joined her, and the desolate look on his face confirmed her fears. "The horse that Finn rode," Rainshadow said. "It too is gone. What can he be doing?"

"You know what he's doing." Jena's voice was distant, mournful. "Going his own way, doing what he thinks he must do. As he's done for a long time now, looking for me. He blames himself for bringing The Claw to the Wasteland, and for leaving his friend. And I know he was hurt and confused by what I said before the council." She shook her head bleakly. "He's been alone all his life, Rainshadow, in a way. That's why it isn't easy for him to think of joining a group like ours. Josh used to say he's a wild creature, but he's not a herd creature."

Rainshadow nodded grimly. "I will take the scouting party out at once – and look for him as well."

"I'm riding with you," Jena said, in a tone that forbade argument.

Before Rainshadow could reply, Marakela's deep voice broke in. She had come up to them in time to hear most of what had been said. "You make that a *raidin'* party," she boomed, "an' me an' all the girls'll come too. Maybe we can slow The Claw down some."

"But first we find Finn," Jena said fiercely, "before he tries to fight The Claw all by himself."

11

Enemy Camp

FINN HAD HAD no trouble slipping away through the crowd, which was too occupied with its own fears to notice him. He had taken a pouch of food and a water-bottle from outside someone's tent, also unseen, and had quickly found the horse he had ridden among the corraled herd. By the time Rainshadow and Jena were looking for him, he was over the hilltop, galloping away at full speed.

He still rode awkwardly, but he was unaware of it. He was scarcely aware, consciously, of his surroundings. He let his senses automatically recognize landmarks and pick up the trail that would lead him back to the cleft where Baer had been left – and where he hoped to find the trail of The Claw. Meanwhile his thoughts turned inward, into the anger and self-hatred that was flaming within him.

If that warrior hadn't ridden in, he thought, he might still be sitting at the gathering place, listening to Corwin's crazy ideas, maybe even letting himself be convinced. It had taken the fact of Baer's danger to sweep all that madness away. He knew there could be no place for him in the Wasteland, just as there couldn't be for Baer. They were both lone wolves, not suited for life among crowds of people. He told himself angrily that he should have gone and talked to Baer sooner. Baer would have known.

And now it was too late. Now The Claw had come.

He had no idea what he was going to do, after he had located The Claw's army. It was very likely a trap, but that did not trouble him. All that mattered was that Baer was in danger.

And if Baer was hurt or dead, he promised himself savagely, he would find The Claw and kill him. However he could, whatever the cost.

So he rode on. His instincts told him when to ease the pace, to rest the horse, just as they kept him on the trail, retracing the route that Rainshadow's people had followed. But his journey would be swifter, for his halts were brief. And also, though he did not know it, The Claw's army was advancing steadily towards him. But even so he intended to drive himself and his horse as hard as had the warrior who brought the news of Baer's capture.

By instinct, too, he kept a careful watch on the sky – and his caution was repaid, on the afternoon of the third day of his relentless ride. He spotted a spywing, no more than a distant blemish above the horizon. At once he vanished into the shelter of a profusion of rocks, and there spent an impatient, watchful hour. The spywing did not seem to have seen him, for it was merely circling, apparently going nowhere. And then the reason appeared.

From below the creature's circle, a plume of dust rose, gradually growing larger. It had to be The Claw's force – and Finn realized that the spywing would be concentrating on the terrain immediately around and in front of the small army. And the dust cloud was moving slowly, he guessed, because the afternoon was waning towards sunset, and The Claw would be seeking a sheltered place to camp.

Leaving his tired horse nibbling gratefully at some scraggy brush, Finn slid forward over the rock-jumbled terrain, a look of fierce determination on his face.

By the time full darkness had settled on to the Wasteland, Finn had crept unseen to the edge of The Claw's camp. He lay on a gritty out-cropping, peering at what he could see of the enemy force – and a wild gladness mingled with his wary caution.

Baer was alive. He was sitting with his arms bound behind him, apparently fastened to a metal stake driven into the ground. And he seemed unharmed, for he was sitting upright, glaring around with an expression of total outrage that at another time might have made Finn smile.

But there was little else to smile about. The Claw had set up camp in the midst of what seemed to be a broad, shallow crater. The sides and floor of the crater were crowded with enormous boulders and great mounded heaps of rock, providing a natural fortification. And, as extra precaution, two spywings were aloft, endlessly circling over the camp.

The rocks and the darkness had allowed Finn to approach, and he felt that he could get even closer without being seen by the batwinged sentries. But caution held him where he was. He could not put Baer at greater risk by some wild, reckless attempt at a rescue. And yet he had no other ideas about how he might set Baer free.

Tumbled rocks hid much of the small army from his view, but his ears and nose told him that the main force of Bloodkin were gathered near to where Baer was tied. Finn could hear their growling talk, and smell the stink of their greasy food. More important, they had built a sizeable fire – which gave the light that had revealed Baer's position, but which would also keep him at a distance.

He shifted position noiselessly, sliding round a bulky shoulder of rock. Now he could see more of the camp, including a number of robed humans gathered round a fire of their own, well away from the Bloodkin. As he thought, the People of the Gorge – probably still hoping to be led by The Claw to some promised land. Fury throbbed within him again as he stared at the humans who so willingly committed the ultimate evil, serving the enemies of humanity.

90

They were engaged in one of their strange ceremonies – seated in a circle round their fire, except for a sinewy, balding man who wore the circular pendant that Finn had seen on old Laslo. The bald man stood with arms raised, mumbling in a throaty voice, and only some of the words were audible above the fire's crackle and the noise of the Bloodkin.

"Great One, strengthen our arms . . . sweep away the evildoers . . . claim these lands . . . our home everlasting . . ."

Finn scowled. So The Claw had promised them the Wasteland, once its free inhabitants had been destroyed. His fists clenched with anger – but he tried to quell it. He was not here to fight the battles of the Wasteland. If he could get Baer free, they might be able to draw The Claw after them, so he did not attack the Wasteland people. But that would be all he could do for them, he thought. It would have to be enough.

The fireside ceremony seemed to be ending. All the robed people rose, arms aloft. "Praise him!" they chanted. "Praise him!"

A wave of barking laughter came from the Bloodkin, whom Finn still could not see. "Hoy, worms," one coarse voice shouted, "come'n praise us!"

The balding man whirled, red-faced with rage. "Animals!" he bawled. "Show some respect!"

The Bloodkin laughter grew uglier, mingled now with snarls. One huge hairy creature lumbered into Finn's view, a hand reaching for the knife at its belt. "You the ones need respec'," he growled. "No worm calls the Bloodkin animals!"

The bald man snatched up a barbed spear and stepped forward, eyes blazing. Finn watched with interest, wondering if the fight might spread into a general brawl, distracting everyone enough for him to get to Baer.

But then he blinked, amazed. As if materializing from the air, The Claw was there, looming between the two antagonists, his hairless skin gleaming in the firelight.

"Put the knife away," The Claw told the Bloodkin in his cold, toneless voice. "Or I will break every finger of the hand that holds it."

The knife vanished, and the Bloodkin backed away, naked fear on his savage face. The bald man stepped forward, grinning and fawning.

"Thank y', lord. Them animals always . . ."

He said no more. Finn knew The Claw had moved, but he had seen only a blur, as the terrible talon lashed out. The bald man flew backwards, sprawling on the ground, one side of his face a welter of blood.

"If you must practise your religion," The Claw said icily to the other humans, "do so away from camp. You are here to fight, not pray. And you are *not* here to fight Bloodkin."

As the people cowered, Finn drew back into the deeper shadows, feeling chilled. He had never seen a blow struck with such speed and such ferocious power. Uneasily, he slipped away to look at the rest of the camp, moving with all of his cautious soundlessness.

But if he had looked back, he would have seen The Claw's head suddenly jerk up – nostrils flaring, cold eyes sweeping the darkness.

On the opposite side of the shallow crater, Finn crept among another cluster of rocks and peered out at the third group within this ill-assorted army. The Slavers – apart from the others as always, their four whirlsleds grouped together in the lee of a formation of rock that was strange even for the Wasteland. Great boulders and mighty slabs were loosely heaped on top of one another, on the sloping side of the crater, rising up for many metres in a gigantic, misshapen tower. It was as if some powerful force of nature had set out to pile giant rock upon rock to create something like a monstrous cairn.

And at the foot of the cairn, or tower, next to the whirlsleds, stood one of the weird structures of the Slavers. It was not much bigger than one of the conical tents of Rainshadow's people, but it was more like a dome – though with the disturbing angles and distortions of all Slaver constructions. Its walls seemed to be made of narrow strips of metal, thin enough to tremble slightly now and then, as if something inside had brushed against it. And Finn guessed that it was the aliens' version of a portable dwelling. The Slavers too, in their way, had come equipped for a military camp.

Finn glanced up, on guard against the still circling spywings, then slid forward, intending to inspect the dome from another angle – and hoping that it might spark some idea of how Baer might be rescued. He was lying flat and unmoving at the edge of the tower of piled rocks that rose above the whirlsleds and the dome, when he heard the whisper of sound.

It was a faint slither, as if a few grains of sand had been dislodged. And even Finn's unique hearing might not have picked it up – had it not been only a few strides away from the shadowed rocks where he lay.

He pressed himself against the ground, not daring to breathe, and listened. The sound was not repeated. But a sixth-sense intuition of danger was bristling his neck-hairs and bringing a chill sweat to his skin. He shifted his eyes back and forth, knowing that in darkness movement is more likely to be detected at the edge of the vision. And in a moment he saw what it was that all his instincts were screaming a warning about.

An almost invisible shape loomed up, just a dim silhouette of head and shoulders against the stars, as Finn peered up from ground level. And the height, and the shape of the domed head, could belong to only one person in the camp. The Claw, prowling the rocks, silent and deadly as a hunting panther.

In that brief glimpse, Finn realized that The Claw had not only moved as stealthily as a wild beast, but also had his own sixth sense. Finn had not moved or breathed – yet the shadowed form of The Claw halted, the great head swung from side to side. And then the figure crouched, and vanished.

Panic clutched at Finn's throat. The Claw had sensed the presence of danger – but where was he? There was not a ghost of a sound, not a hint of movement. And Finn knew exactly how a rabbit must feel, huddling terrified into the ground as a fanged and clawed hunter padded invisibly towards it.

It took every scrap of Finn's courage to keep him from leaping, rabbit-like, into a desperate and suicidal flight. He fought his terror, and instead slid his hand silently towards his knife, bracing himself against the moment when The Claw might come swooping like death itself from the darkness.

But before his fingers reached the knife-hilt, the taut silence was broken. Finn heard a rattling clink like moving metal, and a wide beam of light suddenly streamed out across the rocks. The light fell fully upon the crouched figure of The Claw – not facing Finn, but no more than two strides away from where he huddled.

At once The Claw straightened, turning towards the light, and Finn breathed a silent sigh of relief. The shadow of the boulder where he lay kept him hidden, while the burst of light would temporarily impair The Claw's night vision. He relaxed slightly, and heard a burst of sound come from the source of the light. The gargling, clicking language of the Slavers.

The Claw's cold voice replied, in a fair imitation of the sounds. The conversation went on for a few moments – long enough for Finn to creep forward and peer warily around the rock. As he had thought, the light came from the Slavers' dome. Some of the metal strips had been folded back to create a doorway, where a Slaver stood facing The Claw. Behind the alien, Finn glimpsed glittering machinery, and screens with flickering images on them.

But then he ducked back, for The Claw had nodded respectfully and turned away from the Slaver. For a moment The Claw stared around into the darkness – then he shook his head, and strode decisively away across the camp. Finn relaxed even more, gratefully. Whatever the alien had said, it must have been important enough to divert The Claw from his prowling.

Darkness returned as the Slaver closed the gap in the dome wall, and Finn readied himself to move. But then he paused. Across the camp he could hear the raised voice of The Claw — and the words struck Finn like knives.

"The Masters tell me," The Claw was saying, "that spywings in the desert have spotted a small force of riders, no more than twenty, less than a day's march from here."

A burst of jeering, gloating laughter rose from human and Bloodkin throats, quickly silenced by The Claw.

"They are probably scouts," the cold voice went on, "come to look us over. But we will deal with them. I will take the Bloodkin out against them, tonight. It will be a useful exercise in desert fighting."

Human voices murmured with disappointment, mingled with gleeful Bloodkin growls.

"The spywings," The Claw continued, "have located a place where we can draw the riders into a trap, at daybreak. At that time the People of the Gorge will break camp here and resume our planned route, with the Masters. Remember to take good care of our prisoner."

"More trouble'n he's worth," Finn heard a low voice mutter.

"Silence!" The Claw's cold anger threw a deathly stillness over the camp. "Never forget that the Masters are here primarily for the one called Finn. He too will be trapped, and the renegade is the bait. If anything goes wrong, the Masters will be angry." The icy voice grew deep and ominous. "And so will I."

Finn could almost smell the fear that swept through Bloodkin and humans alike. Or perhaps it was his own fear. For as the Bloodkin flung themselves into an uproar of preparation, Finn sank back into the shadows of the rocks to face an impossible decision.

The riders seen by the spywings had to be Rainshadow and

his scouting party. By morning they would be riding into a trap laid with all The Claw's cunning, where more than a hundred Bloodkin would be waiting for them. Finn desperately wanted to reach Rainshadow first, and warn him. At the same time, with The Claw and the Bloodkin out of the camp, his chances of freeing Baer would be greatly improved. But – how could he leave Rainshadow to die while he tried to rescue Baer?

If only there were some way to free Baer *quickly*, he thought, within a few moments of The Claw's departure. Then he and Baer together might be able to reach Rainshadow in time.

Except there were still the People of the Gorge, standing guard. And Finn still had no idea how to get past them, and get Baer away.

Perhaps if he had a view of the whole camp, he thought, to see where the People of the Gorge deployed themselves after the Bloodkin left. With another swift check of the spywings above the camp, he began stealthily to climb up among the jumbled, piled rocks that formed the huge and craggy tower rising above the whirlsleds. It was a nerve-racking climb, with the threat of the spywings and the treacherous abundance of small, loose rocks among the great stack of boulders. But there were also plenty of gaps and crevices, deep-shadowed, where one giant rock lay upon or leaned against another. In moments he had ascended several metres, unseen and unheard, and was crouching under an overhang, surveying the whole crater and the camp it contained.

He saw the Bloodkin already filing away into the darkness, in the wake of a whirlsled – which was certainly The Claw's, and which had probably been placed, before, on the Bloodkin side of the camp. And he saw the People of the Gorge, most of them readying themselves for sleep – and Baer, sitting as before, some metres away from the robed humans, half-slumped now in a posture of glum weariness. And, directly below Finn, the Slavers' whirlsleds and dome were dark and silent.

Finn stared down at them all, desperately striving to think of some way to do – swiftly – what he wanted to do. As he pondered, he leaned for a moment against a huge, angled slab of rock at his side. There was a small grating sound, almost inaudible, as the rock shifted slightly.

He glanced around, and upwards. For a long moment he studied the huge slab, and the rest of the jutting, haphazard stack of rocks above it, up to the top of the looming tower. Again he pushed carefully against the slab he was leaning against, and felt it shift.

He looked down at the camp once more, measuring distances with his eyes. Then, slowly, he began to unwrap his sling. As he did so, he was smiling, with a strange, reckless brightness in his eyes.

12

Devastation

THE SLING WHIRLED, and a stone sped downwards, unseen, to clatter among some loose rubble next to the whirlsleds.

Nothing happened. The Slaver dome remained dark, and not one of the humans seemed to have noticed the sound.

Finn's mouth twisted wryly. Maybe they'll hear this one, he thought. Another stone flew – and there was a smothered clang, as it ricocheted from the metallic side of a whirlsled.

That sound did have an effect. Several of the People of the Gorge came to their feet, peering into the darkness across the camp.

And then the rest of them leaped up, abruptly, fearfully. Because one of their number had suddenly staggered backwards, blood streaming from his face, before crumpling to the ground.

Finn's smile became a grin. That stone had got their attention. Again the sling whirled, and another man collapsed at the feet of his amazed fellows. And yet another stone then clanged against a whirlsled.

"Over there!" the shout rose. With a burst of angry yelling, the People of the Gorge snatched up weapons and surged towards the whirlsleds. They had forgotten Baer and everything else, in their furious rush. The entire mob spread out to lunge and flail through the darkness round the sleds. If an enemy had been there, he would have been found in seconds.

But instead, he was some twenty metres above their heads, heaving with all his strength against a huge, loose slab of rock.

The rock shifted, tilting slightly, with a low grinding rumble that went unheard in the noise of the search below. Again it shifted, as Finn pushed. But then it halted, as if jammed immovably by the weight of the other boulders around and above it.

Despair swept over Finn like a cold wind. Was the idea not going to work after all? Not that it had been anything but a crazy risk from the beginning . . .

Furiously, straining every muscle, he flung his strength against the great slab. For an instant it remained fixed, solid. But then without warning it slid sideways, as if some unseen obstruction had given way.

And above it, other great rocks slid and shifted, and others above them, through all the upper levels of that high, precariously piled tower from which Finn had removed a central prop.

Slowly, inexorably, the top of the tower began to lean, and tilt, and slide.

It might have been that movement that the spywing sentries saw. Or they might have seen Finn himself, more concerned with speed than caution, flinging himself down the side of the towering rock-pile as sure-footed as a mountain goat. In any case, the winged watchers gave their alarm. The side of the Slavers' dome was flung suddenly open, and two of the aliens, carrying heatlances, eyes glittering ice-blue, stalked swiftly out.

By then Finn was sprinting around the outer edge of the crater, and he did not see them emerge. If he had, he would also have seen their narrow heads jerk up, their eyes almost disappearing as the colour shifted to a near-black purple. He would have seen them start to break into an awkward, stiff-legged run – in the same instant as a monstrous rumble made itself heard across the camp.

Only then did the People of the Gorge, still flailing among the whirlsleds, realize that something was wrong. But it was too late. The enormous cairn of rocks that towered above them began to topple over, in a crushing, murderous avalanche.

Finn had gauged the distance well. The vast weight of falling rock descended upon the whirlsleds and the Slaver dome like titanic hammers. The alien machines vanished, crushed and flattened, and with them into the oblivion of that awesome collapse went many of the People of the Gorge.

Finn had expected that the falling rocks would damage the whirlsleds and the dome, and so might keep the humans and the aliens confused and occupied while he made a dash to free Baer. It had been planned as a diversion – but it became a devastation.

Some never-to-be-explained breakage within the alien energy sources, which powered the Slaver machines, released that energy in one colossal explosion. No sooner had the huge mass of rock, from the tower, struck the ground than it was hurled back into the air by that volcanic blast. Even Finn, more than halfway around the camp, had to fling himself full-length behind a sheltering boulder as the air was filled with the lethal shrapnel of metal and rock fragments, hurled in every direction by the eruption.

The People of the Gorge were not so quick, and were much nearer the blast. Those that had not died beneath the avalanche of rock were mown down by the flying rubble. As Finn rose and moved toward the centre of the camp, dazed and shaken by the enormity of the violence he had unleashed, he could not see a single living thing that might have tried to stop him.

But Baer was alive, and unscathed, thanks to a shoulder of rock that had stood between him and the blast. He was sitting tensely, wide-eyed, and his jaw dropped with surprise as Finn came towards him.

"Son," he said hoarsely, "I dunno how you got here, or how you made all that happen. But I'm surefire glad I'm on your side."

Finn smiled shakily as his knife sliced through Baer's bonds. "I don't know what happened, either," he said. "But let's get out of here. We have to get to Rainshadow."

"That figures," Baer nodded. "The scoutin' party. Just gimme a minute." He began to move purposefully towards the shattered wreckage where the Slavers' machines had stood.

"Careful!" Finn said quickly. "There could still be some alive!"

"If any of those humans lived through that," Baer growled, "they'll keep runnin' till they reach the gorge. But some Bloodkin's got my machete, an' I need to find me somethin' else. Won't be – hey! Lookit here!"

Finn joined him, and looked. The two Slavers from the dome had managed to escape the falling rock – but not the explosion. Both lay face down in the sand, their heads and limbs ripped apart by the flying rock fragments. And near their outflung hands lay their two heatlances.

"Just what we need," Baer said cheerfully. He scooped up the weapons, and almost idly swung their muzzles upwards. One after another they lashed out their brief, hissing flares of red – and the pair of circling spywings, which Finn had nearly forgotten about, became two short-lived fireballs in the night sky.

"Seem in good workin' order," Baer rumbled. He tossed one of the heatlances to Finn. "I never liked 'em much, but they'll do for a while. Now let's go, wherever you've a mind to."

They moved away through the darkness at an easy lope, which left Finn enough breath to tell Baer all that had happened since they parted. Baer only just managed to choke back a bellow of delight at the news that Jena had been found. But then, inevitably, he asked the question that troubled Finn most of all.

"Now you've found what you came lookin' for," he asked, "what d'you do next?"

"I wish I knew," Finn muttered. And that led him into a swift outline of the discussion, or argument, he had had with Corwin and Jena.

When he finished, Baer grunted. "That figures. Quite a choice. I can see why you'd want no part of the war. Still – maybe they got a point, about humans havin' to fight the Slavers sometime." He grinned dourly. "An' it's not much crazier'n what we been doin', tryin' to fight 'em by ourselves."

"That's not the same," Finn said with irritation. "You sound like you agree with them."

"I dunno," Baer shrugged. "It needs some thinkin' about."

With that he fell silent, and Finn gloomily turned his attention back to their surroundings. At least it was not difficult to track the Bloodkin force, even in the dim starlight. And Finn could see that they were not moving at any great speed, so he was confident that he and Baer would be able to overtake them.

But he was also keeping a wary eye on the darkness ahead – which was just as well. The roar of the mighty explosion, back at the camp, had carried a long way in the still desert night. And a moment came when Finn and Baer had to duck into the shadows of some thorny brush as The Claw's whirlsled hummed past, only metres away, speeding back to the camp to find out what had happened.

"Maybe he'll figure the rocks fell by accident," Baer said hopefully, as the sled vanished over the crest of a dune.

"Maybe he won't," Finn replied. "He'll read the signs – and he'll know you didn't get away by yourself. Come on."

Baer sighed and followed, noticing that Finn had quickened the pace. So the hours, and the kilometres, flowed past. At last a greyness began to filter into the eastern sky, soon tinged with the ruddy streamers of approaching sunrise. And soon afterwards Finn came to a halt, head raised to sniff the early morning breeze.

"Just ahead of us," he whispered. "Probably waiting for The Claw."

"Or layin' their ambush."

"Maybe." Finn sniffed again. "We'll move up on them, and find somewhere that you can hide and watch."

"That figures," Baer growled. "I get parked in some more rocks while you go lookin' for the riders."

"Right." Finn smiled. "And *this* time, try not to get caught."

"Wasn't my fault before," Baer grumbled. But Finn was already moving away, as the dawn light spread across the desert.

They crept forward more carefully now, keeping in cover. Around them the landscape remained as ruggedly forbidding as ever, an undulating surface of jutting hills and ridges, separated by steep-sided gullies, defiles and canyons. The usual scatterings of rock outcrops and clusters of great boulders provided the cover they needed, as they crept to the top of one of the uprearing ridges. Below them, a hillside sloped downwards, covered with more rocks and sparse patches of brush. It led down to the broad, sandy floor of a sizeable canyon, with its opposite hillside just as well provided with natural cover.

And both hillsides were swarming with Bloodkin.

Finn and Baer slid into a crevice between two bulky masses of stone, and stared down at the savage horde. The creatures seemed relaxed and idle, yet Finn could see that they were well positioned behind good cover. Anyone entering the canyon and looking *up* at the hillsides would see only rocks and brush.

So this was the place of the ambush – where more than a hundred Bloodkin, all with heatlances, waited for twenty unsuspecting humans.

"They're sure loaded up for war," Baer said softly, his fist clenching on the heatlance he carried. Then he stiffened. "Look! That's the crittur who's got my machete!"

He was pointing to a group lounging among dense brush

directly below them, where one hulking Bloodkin was brandishing Baer's machete. He was clearly making some joke, and the grunting laughter of the others carried clearly up the hillside to Finn and Baer.

"Keep laughin', fella," Baer growled. "Till I come an' shove that blade down your throat."

Finn jabbed him with an elbow. "You stay put," he hissed, "while I go and look for Rainshadow. And if The Claw comes back, keep your head *down*."

Baer scowled, but nodded. And Finn moved off, drifting invisibly among the rocks and brush on the crest of the ridge. In moments he was out of sight of the canyon, and running smoothly in his distance-eating lope.

He planned to make a wide circle around the canyon, hoping that he would spot Rainshadow and the others in time. He was also keeping a careful watch, his heatlance ready, for spywings and for the returning whirlsled of The Claw. But it was neither of those that halted him, some two kilometres from where he had left Baer, and sent him soundlessly into cover among tumbled boulders on the side of a steep bank.

He had heard the unmistakable sound of heavy boots, running at speed towards him.

In a moment the owners of the boots came into view. Four Bloodkin, lumbering rapidly along – and heading, Finn saw, back towards the canyon where the Bloodkin force lay in waiting. The four were glancing back over their shoulders now and then as they ran, but they did not seem troubled. In fact, all four were grinning evilly.

Finn guessed at once what was happening. As the four Bloodkin moved past the bank and disappeared from sight, he lunged forward, intending to launch himself into a wild dash in the direction the foursome had been coming from.

But he had taken only a single stride when he heard the muffled thunder, and saw the first swirls of dust.

And into the hollow at the foot of the steep bank where Finn stood, appeared about twenty human riders, bent low over their horses' necks, galloping in pursuit of the four Bloodkin.

Clearly The Claw had ordered the foursome to find the riders and then to show themselves, at a distance, before turning and running. And the bait had been taken. The riders would be led, unsuspecting, into that narrow canyon, and into the deadly crossfire of the main Bloodkin force.

For a paralysed moment Finn stared at the hurtling riders, recognizing Rainshadow in the lead, with the broad-shouldered form of Marakela next to him. Both of them were carrying heatlances, as were several of the others – no doubt from the small store of the alien weapons that Corwin had mentioned. But Finn's attention was more closely fixed on the small, tanned rider just half a stride behind Marakela.

Even at full gallop over rough ground, Jena was riding as if she had been born to it, as if she were glued to the horse's back. She had even released the reins, guiding her mount only with her knees, while her hands smoothly fitted an arrow to the string of her short bow.

Then the instant of paralysis ended. As the riders thundered nearer, below the slope where he stood, Finn raised the heatlance he was carrying, and took careful aim.

13

Springing the Trap

THE HEATRAY PAINTED a thin red stripe across the morning air, and struck a small rock about five metres in front of the hurtling riders. The suddenly heated stone split across with a crack, splinters spraying from it.

The riders had been a tightly bunched unit – but as the heatray struck, they sprayed out in all directions like the fragments of stone. Dragging their horses into a sliding halt, they leaped for the cover of outcroppings or thickets. It was a skilled, high-speed manoeuvre – and the amazed Finn knew that, had he been an enemy, he might have got off only one more shot before the targets disappeared from sight.

But it was time to let the riders know he was not an enemy.

"Rainshadow! It's me – Finn!"

"*Finn?*" Two voices, Rainshadow and Jena. "Was that you shooting at us?" Rainshadow's voice alone, sounding a little aggrieved.

Finn ran down the slope towards the warriors who were warily emerging from cover. "I had to stop you in a hurry," he explained as he came up to Rainshadow. "You wouldn't have heard me if I'd shouted."

Rainshadow nodded, looking puzzled. "Why stop us?"

"You were riding into a trap," Finn told him. Quickly he described the ambush, and how it had come to be there.

Rainshadow looked even more aggrieved at the news that

they had been spotted. "None of us saw a spywing. We thought The Claw was a day's march away, and the four Bloodkin were just scouts."

"Finn," Jena broke in worriedly, "what happened? With Baer?"

Finn smiled cheerfully. "He's fine. I left him in the canyon, keeping an eye on the Bloodkin." His smile grew a little self-conscious. "I had some luck last night, and . . . well, The Claw's army isn't what it used to be."

He gave them the barest outline of the destruction of The Claw's camp, but it was enough to send the entire group into openmouthed silence – except Jena, who began giggling with a mixture of astonishment and delight.

"Stone me," Marakela grinned, "we might's well go on home an' let this kid fight the war by hisself."

Rainshadow smiled. "Or we can ask him to join us, and hope that he brings his luck with him. We don't want to disappoint those Bloodkin."

"Not a chance," Marakela boomed. "Let's go trap the trappers."

Now it was Finn's turn to be openmouthed. "What are you talking about? You're five times outnumbered!"

Rainshadow shrugged. "An ambush can work both ways. We can at least cut down their numbers before we pull back."

"If we do it right," Marakela added, "we can make a stab at gettin' 'em all."

Finn shook his head numbly. "You're crazy. It's as suicidal as . . . as your idea of starting a war against the Slavers."

"All part of the same war, kid," Marakela growled. "You with us?"

"I said it before," Finn replied stubbornly. "It's not my fight. And it wouldn't be yours, if you had any sense – because it's not a fight you can win."

"Win or lose," Rainshadow said quietly, "it's what we must do."

"Jena . . . ?" There was desperation in Finn's voice.

"Don't say it, Finn," Jena replied firmly. "I'm one of Marakela's riders – that's all. If there's a chance we can reduce The Claw's army, and drive him out of the Wasteland, we have to take it."

"If we don't stop jawin'," Marakela broke in, "the Bloodkin'll come lookin' for us."

Rainshadow gestured, and the riders turned towards their horses. But Finn stepped swiftly in front of Jena.

"I can't let you . . . " he began.

"You can't stop me," she said. "Just like I can't force you to join us."

"At least come with me now," Finn pleaded. "While I go back for Baer."

"All right," she agreed. "But you won't change my mind. This fight has to happen, Finn – and I'm going to be in it."

A short while later, Finn slid silently through the brush on the crest of the hillside above the canyon where the Bloodkin were hidden. Rainshadow and the others had held back for a moment, to let Finn rejoin Baer – so that none of them would mistake Baer for an enemy Bloodkin. But Jena was with him, and Finn was impressed by how easily she had kept pace, and by her effortless stealth. But at the same time he remained determined to keep her safe, out of the battle – even against her will, if necessary.

He was still worrying about that problem when they rounded a clump of thornbush and entered the jumble of massive rocks where Baer waited. The big Bloodkin greeted them with a huge grin that was aimed mostly at Jena. But her answering smile was visibly nervous.

"Mighty glad to meetcha at last," Baer rumbled softly. He thrust out a huge, hairy paw, and his eyes twinkled as he noted Jena's instinctive flinch. "I take some gettin' used to," he added, "but I'm one of the good guys."

"I know you are," Jena said at once, taking his hand in a firm grip. "Don't be offended. I know what you mean to Finn, and what you've done for him, and for me. I hope we'll be friends."

"That we will," Baer grinned. "An' I'm not offended. When Finn an' me first met, he went for my throat like a wild crittur."

"He never did have any manners," Jena replied, her own eyes twinkling. And then she and Baer were struggling to smother their laughter, and grinning at each other as if they had been friends for years.

"If you two could pay attention," Finn broke in, a little testily, "there's a war starting here."

The words wiped the smiles away. And so did the sound that could be clearly heard, as Baer and Jena turned, taking a firm grip on their weapons.

The drumming sound, very near, of galloping hooves.

During Baer and Jena's meeting, Finn had been watching the Bloodkin, who were growing restless and suspicious at the absence of any pursuers of the four Bloodkin, who had been back with the main force for some minutes. But now, as they heard the oncoming horses, there was a stir of readiness among them. Finn saw the group directly below, clearly visible from his vantage point, grin at each other gleefully.

Then the horses burst into the canyon, pounding across its open, sandy floor.

Many of the Bloodkin lunged partly out from their hiding places, to seek a clear aim. A few even fired, in a ragged volley of heatrays.

But no humans fell – because the horses had no riders.

Instead it was Bloodkin who fell, roaring, screaming, dying. A storm of arrows, spears and several heatrays had burst, miraculously, from what had seemed to be the totally deserted upper slopes of both hillsides, above the Bloodkin's hiding places.

In Finn's wake, the Wasteland warriors had silently and

invisibly moved up and over the brows of both hills, taking position above the Bloodkin's exposed backs. Then one of Rainshadow's men had whipped the horses into a stampede, driving them into the canyon to draw the Bloodkin's attention.

Had The Claw been there, his uncanny senses might have spotted the counter-ambush. But in his absence it had worked perfectly. Even the horses had fled unscathed across the open ground. And nearly twenty Bloodkin had fallen in that first attack, without the loss of a single human.

But the remaining Bloodkin were seasoned fighters. Almost at once they recovered from their shock, and dived for cover. From there they began a steady, withering fire into the brush and rocks on the slopes above them. And there were still only twenty humans to return that fire.

Yet they were humans who moved like ghosts into new positions, who slid unseen among rocks and brush to pick off the exposed flanks of the enemy. Sometimes their deadly arrows or heatrays would leap out from spots that did not seem to offer enough cover to hide a rabbit. And most of them found their targets. Slowly, one at a time, the Bloodkin force was being whittled down.

But Rainshadow's people were also suffering losses. In one place a Bloodkin heatray shattered a thin spire of rock, and Finn saw two warriors behind it stagger and fall, their faces turned to masks of blood from fragments of stone. Elsewhere, another heatray turned a clump of brush into an inferno, and from it stumbled one of Marakela's women, hair and clothing ablaze. But even as more heatrays cut her down, she had released a final arrow that buried itself for half its length in a Bloodkin throat.

So the unequal combat went on. And by then Baer had joined in. During the first surprise attack by the humans, Baer had raised his own heatlance and scythed its deadly ray across the group of Bloodkin directly below them. Then he had recklessly plunged down the slope, ignoring Finn's yell. Heatrays had flashed around him, yet he dived unharmed behind the rocks where the Bloodkin had hidden. And he was bellowing a joyous battlecry as he waved up the slope at Finn, flourishing the machete that he had reclaimed.

But by then Finn was no longer watching him. Jena had begun to move as well, and Finn – not knowing what else to do – had grasped her arm in a fierce restraining grip, which had caused her to lose her temper.

"I didn't come all this way to find you," Finn said defensively, "just to see you get killed out here."

Jena's eyes blazed. "Finn, I'm not a little girl now. I've probably seen more battles these past months than you have. I'm not letting Marakela and the others fight this one without me!"

With surprising strength, she jerked her arm free and was gone, a small brown blur vanishing down the slope, leaving Finn feeling anxious, uncertain and more than a little foolish.

But whatever happened, he knew he could not let Jena go into battle without him. Almost before he realized it, he too was moving, angling sideways along the slope, gesturing to Baer to indicate his direction.

By then the Bloodkin had begun a slow, organized withdrawal, making for the edge of the open ground at one end of the canyon, where a substantial collection of bulky boulders offered a refuge. Finn guessed that they had realized they could not compete with the wilderness skills of their enemies on the slopes above them. But if they reached the boulders, they would have a natural fortification, and the small force of humans would have no hope of besieging them.

Finn increased his pace – and as he did so, a heatray flashed past, only centimetres from his shoulder. But the Bloodkin who had fired it did not duck back into cover quickly enough. Finn's heatlance blazed in response, and the Bloodkin fell back, howling, his torso aflame. And Finn moved grimly on, searching for Jena.

But it was growing more difficult to see clearly. Around him

111

the wild battle-scene had grown as lurid as some infernal vision. Both hillsides seemed to be on fire, as the clusters of brush were set alight by the heatrays. The flames roared, choking smoke billowed through the canyon, and crackling heatrays flung a blood-red glow as they sliced and criss-crossed through the air.

Here and there Finn glimpsed shadowy figures flitting through the smoke, and recognized Rainshadow among them from a glimpse of a white stripe of paint across a copper-brown face. The Indian seemed also aware of what the Bloodkin were planning, and was marshalling his own force to cut the enemy off before they could reach the great mass of rocks. But there seemed to be no more than eight humans around Rainshadow, and Finn felt a surge of fear. None of them was Jena – and he could not see any other human warriors, anywhere on the slopes.

He ran on, crouching and weaving among the heavy wafts of smoke. The Bloodkin heatlances fired steadily, covering their withdrawal. They were now only a few metres from the cluster of rocks. Again Finn increased his speed, wishing for a wild moment that he had a Slaver whirlsled at his disposal. Not that he knew how to drive one – but he did know that the more powerful heat-weapons on the sleds were able to blast through most sorts of obstruction.

His mouth twisted in a wry comment on his own thought. The last thing he wanted just then was a whirlsled. Because the only functioning sled in the area, as far as he knew, belonged to The Claw . . .

As the thought entered his mind, it was almost instantly driven out. Earth and stone erupted almost at his feet, in a monstrous, flaming blast. Finn was flung aside like a twig in a wind by the explosion. And when he struggled up, half-stunned, bleeding from the cuts and grazes left by flying shards of rock, he stared down the slope with disbelieving horror.

It was as if his own thought had been turned, by some dark magic, into reality.

Into the open ground of the canyon floor, nosing past the mounded rocks where the Bloodkin were massing, came the whirlsled of The Claw – its mighty heatray sweeping across the hillside in a broad, fiery swathe of destruction.

14

Fury of The Claw

IF THE BATTLEGROUND had been lurid before, it was now entirely hellish. The whirlsled, still creeping slowly out on to the canyon floor, did not leave a trail of burning brush behind it, as did the lighter heatlances. Where its lethal ray swept, bushes were simply incinerated, leaving nothing but blackened ash drifting away with the smoke. And where it focused its full power on a rock outcropping, the rock also vanished in an explosive blast like the one that had felled Finn.

But now Finn's dazed senses were clearing, enough to see that the tide of battle had turned. The guerrilla tactics of Rainshadow's people had been able to drive the Bloodkin back, and reduce their numbers – but they would have no effect on The Claw. The upper part of a whirlsled's hull was impervious even to heatlances, Finn knew, so spears and arrows would be useless. Or worse than useless – for as Finn watched, the terrible ray struck at a cluster of rocks from which a spear had just hurtled. And the blast flung not just rock fragments into the air, but also the torn and flaming body of one of Rainshadow's men.

Something close to panic seized Finn. He knew that if The Claw and his whirlsled had been with the Bloodkin force at the outset, the battle might never have been begun. Now that he had finally rejoined his forces, it was clear that the battle could not be won.

Over the crackling flames and the explosive firing of the whirlsled's weapon, Finn could hear the savage, gloating yells of the Bloodkin. They had halted their retreat, and seemed to be waiting for something – perhaps a signal from The Claw, that would hurl them into a massed charge against what was left of the small human force. Finn had no idea how many still lived, for all of them had now disappeared, seeking cover from the murderous assault of the whirlsled. Desperately, certain that the battle would be lost in only moments, Finn sprinted across the smoke-veiled slope, shouting Jena's name.

He could scarcely hear his own voice above the din of battle. But then he caught sight of her, farther down the slope. For a heart-stopping moment he thought she was dead, for she lay face down and unmoving behind a ridged slab of rock. But as he raced towards her, she raised her head slightly and slid forward half a metre, as if to peer round the slab.

Finn was about to shout again, but instead he came to a crouching halt, raising his heatlance. He had glimpsed, through the smoke, the outline of a huge, shaggy body. But then he looked again, and relaxed. It was Baer, calmly resting on one knee, apparently fiddling with the heatlance that he held.

Finn knew that Baer was able to take the slim tubes apart in order to replace the alien power source within them, when one was exhausted. But he could not imagine what Baer was doing now. Even if his lance's charge had run out, where could he have got a spare? Yet for some reason he had separated the lance into its two halves, and was probing into its interior.

Before Finn could move again, Baer rejoined the two segments of the lance, and rose to his feet. Careless of the fact that he was totally exposed, he started down the slope – running in a heavy gallop straight for The Claw's whirlsled.

Finn stared, aghast. In a moment Baer was less than twenty metres from the sled – which was then concentrating its fire on the opposite slope. As he ran, Baer drew back the hand that was gripping the heatlance – gripping it by one end, like a club.

Then he threw it, in a looping, spinning arc, towards the sled.

No one needed to tell Finn about Baer's skill at throwing the machete, which was shorter than the heatlance but slightly heavier. Now that same skill dropped the heatlance neatly on to the ground in front of the whirlsled, which was still continuing its slow advance.

Some part of Finn's dazed mind realized that Baer must have done something to the power source within the lance that would, with luck, turn it into an explosive. He watched, rooted to the ground, as the sled crept forward, and the thrown heatlance vanished from view beneath its underside, where the cushion of energy held it half a metre off the ground.

Then several things happened at once.

The sled's heat-weapon swung round with frightening speed, towards Baer, who was dashing back to the safety of the rocks.

The red flare of the ray scorched from its muzzle, just as Baer tried to fling himself behind a pile of stony rubble far too small to shelter his bulk.

The vicious ray struck – and Baer was flung away, spinning and rolling on the canyon floor, one entire side of his body erupting into flame.

And even as the ray found its target, from under the whirlsled came the thunderous roar of an explosion. The sled was thrown upwards by the blast, its energy cushion disrupted, and toppled with a grinding crash on to its side.

For Finn, staring at the motionless, smouldering body of his friend lying face down in the dust, everything seemed to come to a halt. He barely heard the explosion of the lance. He did not hear Jena's horrified scream, nor the roars of shock and rage from the Bloodkin. His vision blurred, as if something had flung a shadow – a red shadow – across his eyes. Then he could see again, in a strange focused way, as if he was looking down a tunnel of light with only reddened darkness all around.

In the centre of that narrow focus, he saw The Claw.

The tall, hairless man seemed unhurt by the wreck of his

116

whirlsled. He crawled slowly from the broken machine and rose to his feet, blinking dazedly.

Finn was not aware that he had started running. He did not even glance at Jena as he raced past her. He did not see her start to reach out to him, then flinch back, wide-eyed and suddenly pale. For in that flashing glimpse, she had not seen a human being. She had seen a beast, or a devil.

Dried streaks of blood stood out starkly against the death-white pallor of Finn's face. His skin was stretched taut across his cheekbones, his lips writhed back from his teeth in a snarl, his eyes blazed with a savage fire. Whatever part of Finn Ferral was a wild animal, that part had taken control – and had run amok.

Like a rabid wolf, like a maddened mountain lion, Finn hurtled out on the canyon floor, and launched himself at The Claw.

Only the unhesitating, manic ferocity of that attack saved Finn's life. Though The Claw was still slightly off balance from the wreck of the whirlsled, the evil talon of his left hand struck a flashing, defensive blow that was so swift as to be almost invisible. It might have torn half of Finn's face away. But The Claw had misjudged Finn's own speed – so that it was the muscled forearm, not the talon, that crashed against the side of Finn's head.

Even so, the blow hurled Finn off his feet, slamming him into the unyielding metal of the overturned whirlsled. As he slid half-stunned to the ground, shock and pain had restored him to himself. He was no longer a berserk beast. He was a human being again, who knew he had started a fight he could not hope to win.

The Claw stepped forward, towering over him. Finn looked up at the hairless dome of the man's head, streaked with dust – saw the jutting cheekbones beneath the glaring, deep-set eyes –

saw the cruel mouth twisted into a grimace that might have been a grin of triumph. For a moment Finn felt that he was looking at a skull, a death's head. But it was his own death, he knew, that was foreshadowed.

The Claw moved again, and Finn scrambled backwards, rising unsteadily to his feet. In his frenzied charge down the slope, the maddened beast that he had become had had no thought for weapons. Somewhere along the way he had dropped and lost his heatlance. Now, though he knew it would not be enough, though he felt the sweaty grip of panic threatening to engulf him, Finn drew his knife, and waited.

Around him, the noise of battle had faded. The wrecking of the sled, the fall of Baer, Finn's wild attack – all seemed to have imposed silence on the other combatants, as if time itself had been suspended.

The Claw's cold voice cut through the breathless stillness. "I suspect that you know nothing of the arts of combat." He took another menacing step forward. "You might profit from this lesson – were it not to be your last."

Fighting the panic, Finn took a grip on his courage. Though the moment of insane fury had passed, some part of him was still, as always, a wild creature. And at this moment he was a trapped, cornered wild creature.

Without warning, he sprang at The Claw, striking upwards with his glittering blade at the black-clad torso.

But the knife stabbed only empty air.

Finn's attack had been swift, but The Claw's speed was beyond belief. Smoothly he had twisted aside, and in the same motion had slashed down with his taloned hand. Blood gouted from a great gash in Finn's forearm, and the knife fell from his grasp. And even before the knife struck the ground, The Claw had pivoted, and swung a leg in a ferocious, sweeping kick.

Again Finn was lifted from the ground, flung metres away into a crumpled heap. His torn right arm was on fire, and more agony speared through his upper body, where the terrible kick

118

had surely cracked some ribs. He lay there, gasping, fighting to clear his vision, as The Claw stalked coldly towards him.

Instinct alone forced him to move, at the last second. He rolled to one side, grunting with the pain of the movement, as The Claw's boot flashed towards him again. Had the kick landed, it would have shattered his shoulder. But instead Finn was able to drag himself to his feet, swaying, to confront his enemy.

"Excellent." The Claw's mocking laugh held the sound of breaking ice. "You show promise – and a foolish courage. But it will not be enough."

Again the ugly talon lashed out at Finn's face. Finn tried to dodge it, then realized too late that it was a feint. The Claw's other hand, rigid as an axe-blade, chopped down at the left side of Finn's neck. And in the same instant of flowing motion, another kick had swept Finn's feet from under him.

He fell heavily, crying out with the pain. The chopping edge of that hand had crushed his collar-bone, numbing his uninjured left arm. A wave of darkness rose out of the pain, seeking to drag him down to unconsciousness. But again his instincts took charge, forcing him to roll away, to roll again and again, though he was sobbing from the grinding agony of his wounds.

And The Claw stalked him, still with his death's-head grin. Finn stared up, barely able to focus his eyes, knowing that he had only seconds left.

But The Claw halted. "I am not going to kill you, of course." The cold tones were almost conversational. "The Masters would never forgive me. But they will repair any damage I do to you. And I owe you some pain, young fool, for all the trouble you have caused me."

His booted foot struck out, with rattlesnake speed. Finn could not have avoided the kick by reflexes alone. But he had not even been looking. He had already begun another desperate roll to one side – so the boot that should have found the pit of his stomach merely glanced bruisingly off his hip.

Even so, the power of it sent him skidding away over the dry sand. He came to rest against some obstacle. Vaguely, through the waves of lancing pain that were dimming his mind, he was aware that the obstacle was soft, and somehow sticky. Then at the edge of his vision he saw a tangled, furry yellowishness.

He was half-lying across the motionless body of Baer.

A swift glance showed him that one side of Baer's body was a mass of scorched flesh and seeping blood, which had spread in a sticky pool around and under him. And the sight struck Finn like a cold and cleansing wind, galvanizing what was left of his strength. As The Claw again strode unhurriedly towards him, he struggled to raise himself, aware that some feeling was returning to his numbed left arm.

But he had managed to reach only a half-sitting position when The Claw's shadow fell across him.

"Did you imagine the renegade would come back to life and aid you?" the icy voice laughed. "No – there is no aid for you, nor for the fools who came here with you. And now it is time to end this enjoyable interlude."

Finn had barely listened to the words, and had stopped struggling to rise. Not because he had given up – but because he had seen something, behind the looming form of his enemy. Something small and brown and lithe, moving swiftly, soundless as a puff of dust.

Jena – her face contorted into a mask of rage and determination, and her hunting knife gleaming in her hand.

In the instant that The Claw began to reach for Finn, Jena took three silent, running strides, and sprang. She seemed to run up the towering back of The Claw like a cat up a tree. Then she hung there for a frozen fraction of a second, knife poised.

But The Claw's reactions were equal to the danger. Jena's weight had pulled him slightly off-balance – yet before her knife descended, he struck upwards and back, with his taloned hand. The evil curved point flashed a centimetre away from Jena's

120

face, and the side of the talon slammed against her forehead, hurling her backwards and away.

Grimly The Claw began to turn towards her, talon raised. Jena was sprawled on the ground, dazed and helpless. And that helplessness, the certainty that she was a second from death, injected a last flush of adrenalin into Finn's damaged body, and a final echo of his battle madness.

Ignoring the grating agony of his broken ribs and collarbone, he lunged across the shaggy, motionless back of Baer – reaching towards the machete that had been reclaimed, jerking it from its sheath.

The Claw sensed the movement, and whirled. Snarling, he slashed down at Finn with the murderous talon – at precisely the moment that Finn swung the machete upwards in a desperate, frenzied sweep.

Weapon met weapon with a dull, crunching clang. And with the force of the impact, the razor edge of Baer's machete sheared effortlessly through flesh and bone.

The Claw staggered back, howling like an injured beast, staring with glazed disbelief at the hooked shape of his severed left hand rolling in the dust, and the blood fountaining from the stump of his wrist.

And as he howled and stared, Finn dragged himself to his knees, and surged upwards, plunging the glittering blade nearly its full length into The Claw's unprotected chest.

15

Family

HE WAS CROSSING the continent again. But this time he was doing so at a great height, moving at incredible speed on unseen wings. Below him, forests and lakes and rivers and plains rushed by, as he swept above them. It was night, starless and dark, yet he could see every detail of the ground – every leaf, every thorn, every pebble. He was soaring now above the rugged, broken landscape of the Wasteland, and his gaze penetrated into the depths of a rocky canyon. Near the edge of the canyon floor lay Baer, face-down and still, with blood gushing from the ghastly destruction of his side. The blood seemed to be endless, pouring out around Baer's unmoving body, spreading until it became a wide pool, then a small lake that filled the canyon. He felt his invisible wings falter and droop. He was plunging downwards towards that dark pool. And as the dive began he saw the towering figure of The Claw, striding miraculously over the surface of the pool. Frantically he tried to change direction, but it was impossible. The effort brought grinding pain, tearing at his arms, his shoulder, his chest. And now The Claw was standing over Baer, waiting for him, grinning his death's-head grin, raising the terrible hooked talon. He could feel the ice-cold point of it trailing across his face. . . .

"Finn?"

He opened his eyes.

Jena was sitting beside him, smiling down a little nervously. He stared at her for a moment without recognition, without understanding why she was stroking his forehead with a damp, cool cloth. Then he shifted slightly on the bed of soft hides, and the stabs of pain throughout his body brought all the rest of his mind back into the full misery of remembering.

"Lie still," Jena said. "You mustn't thresh around."

"How . . . " His voice came out in a croak, and Jena reached for a container of water, held it for him to sip. "How long has it been?" he said at last.

"You've been unconscious for nearly two days," Jena said. "We were very worried."

Finn raised his head slightly, trying to ignore the flares of pain, and stared down in dismay at the tangle of strappings and bandages that enveloped him. Gently, Jena's cool hand pushed his head back down.

"You're mending well," she said soothingly. "Corwin says everything should heal perfectly. As long as you stay still, and let it heal."

Finn nodded faintly, his gaze drifting away, vaguely registering that he was in one of the conical tents of the Wasteland people. "He *is* dead, isn't he?" he asked. "The Claw?"

"Yes," Jena said quietly. "You killed him."

"Not me," Finn said. "*We* killed him. I didn't have a chance, till you joined in."

Jena smiled. "We'll argue about it when you're better."

"What happened after?" Finn asked. "The Bloodkin . . . and Rainshadow . . . ?"

"It was strange," Jena said, her eyes gazing darkly into an unseen distance. She described how the whole battle had stopped, as if everyone had been paralyzed, while Finn and The Claw fought. And when The Claw fell, the spell was broken. The remaining Bloodkin had run into the cluster of massive rocks that was like a fortress. But Rainshadow had known that

123

they had brought only limited supplies with them, from the camp that Finn had destroyed. So he had simply left them there, with two warriors nearby to keep an eye on them.

"They can either stay there, or make a run for it," Jena said, a fierce edge in her voice. "One way or another, the Wasteland will finish them."

Finn sighed. "So Rainshadow is alive?"

"Oh, yes. He was injured, but he's up and walking. And there were five others who survived, though they'll all carry scars." Jena smiled suddenly. "All except Marakela. Somehow she came through the whole thing without even a cut or a bruise."

Finn glanced at her, aware for the first time of the marks on her smooth arms and legs where rock splinters had gashed the skin. His eyes drifted up to the discolouration of her forehead – the bruise, now fading, left by The Claw's last blow.

A cold shiver swept down his spine, and he turned away. He had another important question to ask, and he dared not look at Jena while he asked it.

"Have . . . " His throat seemed to close for a moment, but he tried again. "Have they buried Baer?"

"Buried . . . " Jena's voice sounded oddly strained. "Oh. No – not yet."

"Good." Finn shut his eyes, willing his voice not to break. "I wanted to be there. I thought . . . we might take him to that oasis. I think he'd like that."

Again Jena's voice sounded stifled, as if she were choking back tears. "I don't . . . I don't honestly think he would."

"Dam' right," said a rich bass voice from across the tent. "Stop tryin' to rush a fella inta the ground."

Finn's eyes flew open, and he snapped his head around, not noticing the flare of pain from his collar-bone. Jena was not fighting back tears, but laughter. And filling the doorway of the tent was a huge, oddly-shaped bulk. Baer – the whole of his massive upper body swathed in bandages.

"You're alive!" Finn gasped.

"Sure am," Baer grinned. "It was close, a while there – but your pal Corwin knows some good tricks."

"But the heatray . . . " Finn spluttered. "I saw you, burning . . . "

"Yep," Baer agreed, "but it wasn't as bad as it looked. The ray just grazed me, so it took skin an' a bit of meat – an' set my hair on fire. But then it knocked me rollin', which put out the fire. Put me out, too, so I musta looked pretty dead, lyin' there bleedin'. But there's lotsa blood where that came from."

As if to prove the point, he slapped himself firmly on the chest, then winced ferociously. Finn didn't know whether to laugh or cry, but it didn't matter, since he was already doing both – smiling shakily, while his eyes filled with tears of thankfulness and relief.

But he blinked them back as others crowded into the tent behind Baer's bulk. Rainshadow, wearing a bandage in place of his headband, one arm supported in a sling, but grinning merrily. And with him the small rotund form of Corwin, and big red-headed Marakela, their faces also wreathed in smiles.

"So you have decided to live after all?" Rainshadow said to Finn.

"Just barely," Finn replied.

"That will do for now," Corwin laughed. "In a week or so, you will be up and ready to do it all over again."

Finn shook his head faintly. "Don't count on it."

"Should we not?" Rainshadow's voice had grown serious. "You told us that our fight was not your fight. Yet you came to warn us of the ambush. And you and Baer joined the fight, and turned it in our favour, when you might easily have gone your own way."

Finn looked defensive. "I couldn't let you ride into a trap. And in the canyon I couldn't leave Jena. But that's not the same thing as . . . as your crazy idea of making war on the Slavers."

"Is it not?" Corwin put in, earnestly. "Think, Finn. You say that you joined the battle in the canyon for the sake of your sister. We want to fight the Slavers for the sake of the human race. There is no difference. While the Slavers rule Earth, *all* humans are brothers and sisters – united in the same conflict."

Finn looked away. As before, at the place of the council, Corwin's words were confusing and bewildering him. He was sure that the little man was wrong, but he could not find a way to make his feeling clear, even in his own mind.

"And think of this, as well," Corwin went on. "You have fought the Slavers, *alone*, and have won victories greater than any band of Wasteland warriors has managed. Whether it was great skill or unusual luck, I do not know. Perhaps both. But whatever it was, Finn, *we need it*." Corwin leaned forward, eyes shining with fervour. "But also, young man, *you* need *us*. Because a day may come when your skill and luck will not be enough, by themselves – as nearly happened against The Claw. And then you will not want to be . . . *alone*."

Finn remained silent, his mind filling with images. Baer charging the whirlsled – Jena fearlessly leaping at The Claw.

"I know what you're saying," he replied at last. "Maybe I can't hope to go my own way, and live as I want, in this world. But I still think the idea of making war on the Slavers is crazy. Just a way to get you all killed."

Rainshadow shrugged. "Everyone dies, Finn. In the Wasteland, the possibility of death is always a step away. Is it otherwise, in your eastern forests?"

"Finn," Jena put in, "even without The Claw, the Slavers won't stop looking for you. You'd be fighting your one-man war every minute of every day. Wouldn't you be better off with us, with people who care for you, fighting in *our* war?"

His mind in turmoil, Finn slid his eyes across all the concerned, intense faces above his bed. They were all watching him, waiting for his response. Even big Marakela was nodding firmly in agreement, her eyes fixed on him. And Finn began to feel abashed. It seemed to mean so much to them, whether or not he stayed, and became a Wasteland warrior. Yet still he did not know what to say, did not know even what he truly thought, or wanted. So at last he turned his gaze to the one place where he could hope to find some understanding, some kind of answer.

"Baer?"

"Tell you what I figure," the big Bloodkin rumbled. "I figure these folks came here to talk you inta joinin' them, 'cause you matter to 'em. An' you're not even listenin' to 'em too good. If you were, you'd know they're talkin' sense – an' I'll tell you why. It's 'cause they're the kinda folks that could pick *me* up outa my own blood, two days ago, an' cart me back here, an' patch me up, an' look after me as kind an' friendly as if I was one of their own."

"You are," Jena put in firmly.

"Dam' right," Marakela boomed. "Nobody's fergettin' what you did in the canyon."

Baer tugged at his beard, looking pleased. "Yep, well, maybe I am one of 'em, now. An' so're you, Finn, if you'd see it. You been feelin' different an' alone for so long that you got like me, figurin' you'd never find a place where you belong. But *this* is that place, boy. These folks're your folks." He snorted vigorously. "Remember The Claw, back in the gorge, sayin' he was the first of a new race? He was wrong. These folks here, *they're* the new race – a new breed of humans. They're tough, an' brave, an' wilderness-smart. They know how to live together, an' how to help each other. An' they know what's gotta be done, sometime, somehow, about the Slavers. They're *your kind of folks*, Finn – an' mine. So I figure on hangin' round awhile, an' doin' what I can. Not just 'cause I owe 'em – but 'cause I like 'em."

"That's how I feel, too," Jena said softly.

Another silence fell, as Finn again looked from one to another of the faces that gazed down at him. And an odd feeling began to well up within him, somehow constricting his throat, so that he could not have spoken even if he could have found the words.

Once I had a family, he thought. Then they were taken, and I had no one – until I met Baer, and gained a friend. Now it seems that I'm not only going to have my family back, but I could have a whole Wasteland full of friends. Only it felt more like . . . like he was being invited to become part of a vastly larger family.

Corwin had said that they needed him, which was flattering. He also said that Finn needed them – which was not so flattering, but even more true. Jena was right – he might not be able to elude the Slaver's pursuit forever. And anyway, he had done what he had set out to do, to find Josh and Jena. What was there for him to do now?

When the answer to that question came to him, it was blindingly obvious. And with it came another, surprising, realization. It was not simply that there would be no purpose in his life if he went back to the lonely, dangerous existence of the past months. It was that the idea had now, suddenly, become distasteful. Baer's words had sorted through the clouded confusion of his feelings, and made him see that now, after all the violence and desperation of the past days, he did not want to leave these people. As Baer said – they were his people.

The slow grin that appeared on his face brought answering smiles of happiness and relief to the faces of the others. "All right," Finn said. "You're right, and I've been wrong. I suppose I do belong here, if I belong anywhere." His brows knitted in a mock frown. "Why do all of you know me better than I do?"

"'Cause you're just natural-born dumb," Baer rumbled cheerfully. "But you're gettin' smarter."

"And now you must also get better, quickly," Rainshadow put in.

"Why?" Finn asked. "Are you declaring war on the Slavers right away?"

"Not just yet." The reply came from Jena, her eyes bright. "What we're doing first, when you're healed, is having the biggest celebration the Wasteland ever saw."